RED PANDA

# FOLKTALES FROM TAMIL NADU

NARAYAN DEVANATHAN

*For Amma and Appa who taught me that every day can be lived with joy and for my niece Megha, who taught me not to take myself too seriously, ever.*

FOLKTALES FROM

# TAMILNADU

Narayan Devanathan is the youngest of six children born into a Tamil family where traditions were fun as much as fun itself was a tradition. As the kadai kutti (literally 'last little one' but loosely translated as 'the youngest and spoilt one') in the family, he received much pampering from his mother (and his siblings, to an extent). Of all the things he received from his mother though, his absolute favourites are the Tamil folktales she narrated to him, cherished to this day. Giving them form, emotion and colour in the English language—another unreasonably favourite thing of his—has been a joy for him.

His other loves include exploring all kinds of writing (multi-lingual puns, rhyming and free verse, essays, travelogues, humour, young adult fiction and dark satire), long distance running, people watching and dessert (especially Indian sweets and ice cream).

His nomadic journeys across five decades have seen him call numerous places home: Hyderabad, Iowa, New York, Wisconsin and currently, Delhi/NCR.

Published by Red Panda, an imprint of Westland Books, a division of Nasadiya Technologies Private Limited, in 2026

No. 269/2B, First Floor, 'Irai Arul', Vimalraj Street, Nethaji Nagar, Alapakkam Main Road, Maduravoyal, Chennai 600095

Westland, the Westland logo, Red Panda and the Red Panda logo are the trademarks of Nasadiya Technologies Private Limited, or its affiliates.



ISBN: 9789371973168
10 9 8 7 6 5 4 3 2 1

Book Design by Pratik M. Kalekar

This is a work of fiction. Names, characters, organisations, places, events and incidents are either products of the author's imagination or used fictitiously.



Printed at Nutech Print Services Pvt. Ltd

Knock, Knock!

Who's there?

Why did the

frog climb the tree?

Wait, that doesn't make sense.

Because he didn't want

to get wet!

– A reminder from my three-year-old
niece that logic is no match for imagination

# Contents

# Author's Note

Dear Reader,

Regardless of your age, I hope you will be reading this as a child. I will talk as if I'm a child, and I will talk to you as if you are a child.

You see, there's a special power we have when we are children: we know there are no limits to the powers of our imagination. And so, we go on road trips in an aeroplane, we take boat rides into the sky and we ride a scooter on the open ocean, because, why not?

In the worlds of our imagination, storks can be silly, flies can be forgetful, sparrows can be smart, peppers can be princes, kittens can be kids and appams ... oooh, appams! They will always be mouth-watering.

When I wrote these stories, I didn't want to make sense, or teach you morals or tell you how the world works. There are others who will do that and do it much better than I ever can. All I wanted to do was to convey a bit of the magical feeling that explodes in my head when I read stories like these. It's like fireworks go off in my brain but they also taste yummy, like buttery, crunchy murukku crackling away inside your mouth as you chomp down on them.

Oh, and I did want to do one other thing: share the magic that my mother–my amma–shared with me through stories when I was much, much younger. The best way to describe her stories is that they are uniquely Tamil, uniquely amma.

In presenting these stories to you in this book that you now hold in your hands, I have tried to recreate that magic, in English but without losing their Tamil-ness, their amma-ness. I hope you will feel the twinkle in her eye, the chuckle in her laugh, the surprise in her voice when you read these stories. I hope you will be immersed in the uniquely Tamil universe these stories live in.

And for a little while, I hope you will be transported to a different world, beyond logic, beyond rules, where imagination reigns. And I hope you will be tempted to keep returning to that world again and again.

## Ammi Kallu

A traditional grinding stone used to crush and grind spices, chutneys and masalas. It is usually made from natural black granite or other hard stone.

# The Fly Who Forgot His Name

On a hot, sultry morning, a fly sitting on a cow's thick-skinned back suddenly sat up straight.

'I've forgotten my name! Cow, I've forgotten my name! Do you remember my name?'

'I, unfortunately, don't remember your name. Maybe you can ask my calf.'

'Calf of the Cow on whose back I sit, do you remember my name?'

'I do not. Ask the Cowherd who looks after us.'

'Cowherd of the Calf of the Cow on whose back I sit, do you happen to remember my name? I have forgotten it!'

'Oh, no. I'm afraid I can't help you. But you can ask my wooden staff.'

'Wooden Staff of the Cowherd of the Calf of the Cow on whose back I sit, would you at least remember my name?'

'Sorry, I don't. You could ask the branch of the tree from where I came.'

'Branch of the Tree from where came the Wooden Staff of the Cowherd of the Calf of the Cow on whose back I sit, help me please. I have forgotten my name. Do you remember it?'

'Alas, I don't! But you can ask the stork sitting on me.'

'O Solitary Stork on the Branch of the Tree, from where came the Wooden Staff of the Cowherd of the Calf of the Cow on whose back I sit, woe is me for I don't remember my name at all. By some stroke of storks' luck, do you know it?'

'Why, no. But maybe the fish I was about to catch might …'

'O Squeamish Fish, eyed by the Stork on the Branch of the Tree from where came the Wooden Staff of the Cowherd of the Calf of the Cow on whose back I sit, I am at my wits' end, and no one has been able to help. Do you know my name?'

'By my eyelidless eye, I wish I could help, but I do not know your name either. Check with that fisherman, whose clutches I may not escape if I don't become the stork's bill of fare for the night.'

'Handsome Fisherman, closing in on the Fish eyed by the Stork on the Branch of the Tree from where came the Wooden Staff of the Cowherd of the Calf of the Cow on whose back I sit, I am dizzy from my search because I don't know my own name.'

'Don't distract me now. Ask that water urn of mine. He sits around all day doing nothing.'

'Earthy Urn of the Fisherman, fishing for the Fish eyed by the Stork on the Branch of the Tree from where came the Wooden Staff of the Cowherd of the Calf of the Cow on whose back I sit, if you do one thing today, let it be this: remember my name, please?'

'What do I know of such things? Better you ask the potter who shaped me.'

'O Shapely Potter, who shaped the Urn of the Fisherman fishing for the Fish eyed by the Stork on the Branch of the Tree from where came the Wooden Staff of the Cowherd of the Calf of the Cow on whose back I sit, I beg of you to still your wheel for a moment and stir your memory instead. Pray, tell me, what is my name, for I have myself forgotten it.'

'Begone. If I don't craft an exquisite urn for the king by this evening, my name will be dragged through the mud. But there is an idea. Ask the mud instead. For the earth forgets nothing.'

'O Malleable Mud, muse and material for the Potter who shaped the Urn for the Fisherman fishing for the Fish eyed by the Stork on the Branch of the Tree from where came the Wooden Staff of the Cowherd of the Calf of the Cow on whose back I sit, I'm told you forget nothing. I beseech you to remember my name.'

'This grass that has grown all over me has covered my memory too. Why don't you ask it instead?'

'Grass of the Mud of the Potter of the Urn of the Fisherman of the Fish of the Stork of the Branch of the Tree of the Wooden Staff of the Cowherd of the Calf of the Cow on whose back I sit, please don't tell me you don't know my name or have never seen me at all.'

'I can't say that I do. But this horse that pulls at me so uncouthly even as I talk to you ... perhaps he knows.'

'Chomping Horse of the Grass of the Mud of the Potter of the Urn of the Fisherman of the Fish of the Stork of the Branch of the Tree of the Wooden

Staff of the Cowherd of the Calf of the Cow on whose back I sit, I have tired myself wandering and wondering, asking and seeking. Would you be so kind as to tell me my name?'

'Go away, you annoying thing. Can't you see I'm busy with dinner? Pick up your wings and go; away you fly!'

'Fly! Why, that is indeed my name! Thank you so much, O Chomping Horse! Now I can blissfully return to being the Fly on the back of the Cow whose Calf is usually steered by the Cowherd with his Wooden Staff from the Branch of the Tree, where sits the Stork eyeing the Fish, who tries to dodge the Fisherman with the Urn made by the Potter with the Mud on which grows the Grass which you, Chomping Horse, now pull at.'

## Dosa Kallu

Literally meaning Dosa stone, it is a flat cooking pan used to make dosas, uttappams and similar dishes. Traditionally made from soapstone, it holds heat well and cooks evenly.

# The Soothsayer

Once upon a time, there lived a man whose wife fed him only one dosai (a crisp and savoury crepe made of lentils and rice) whenever she made them. But the man had a lingering hunch that she always made more and ate all but one by herself, saving only the last dosai for him.

One day, determined to find out for himself, he told his wife he was going out and would be back in time for dosai at dinner. Instead of leaving the house, he went up to the terrace and hid himself in a corner right above the kitchen.

When his wife started making the dosai, he started counting them. Sssaiiiiin!

'Ah, that's the first dosai, sizzling away on one side,' he counted.

For every two sizzling sssaiiiiins, he counted one dosai. By the time she was done cooking, his wife had made ten dosais. After a while, the man quietly went downstairs through the back door, circled the street and then returned home.

Yennai Chuttade Dosai
Tedi Kudithadu kazhidai
Yertrum iraindade taneer
konni kum mooku...

'Ah, you are just in time for a hot dosai,' his wife greeted him. 'Come, there is enough batter left for one. I will serve it to you just now.'

'Wicked woman!' the man roared. 'I know you are lying. You do not know, but I have the gift of divination—I know you have prepared ten dosais, not just one.'

'Forgive me, swami,' she cried, astounded and alarmed at having been found out. 'I will serve you enough dosais to fill your stomach. You may eat to your heart's content.'

Now, while being chastised for being discovered, the woman was also proud of her husband's soothsaying abilities and went around telling her neighbours and friends about it.

One day, a poor washerman came around to the man with a plea.

'Learned One,' he said, 'my livelihood depends on my donkey, but that wretched creature has gone missing since last night. I have searched high and low but have been unable to find a hide nor hair of the beast. Please use your divine vision and tell me where I can find him.'

Now, the self-proclaimed soothsayer found himself desperately looking for a way out of his predicament. I might as well be a donkey, he thought mournfully to himself, finding myself thus cornered.

Out loud, he said, 'The place of a useless one—as a donkey—is by the corner of the smallest and least useful wall in town.'

The washerman immediately went to the farthest corner of the town and, to his surprise, found his donkey—as prophesied—grazing by a dilapidated wall. But much to his dismay, the soothsayer's fame spread far and wide after this display of his ability.

One day, a farmer came up to his house.

'O Diviner,' he began, 'My crops have been without water for a long time because of the delayed rains. Pray, tell me, when will it rain again?'

The diviner, realising that his non-fortune-telling powers would need to be deployed if he had to make his way out of this episode unscathed, plotted the path forward. He brought out his cowrie shells and scattered them in an elaborate yet random manner. He drew criss-crossed lines around them and closely studied the patterns they formed on the floor.

'You are in luck, Farmer,' he proclaimed. 'It shall rain tonight itself. Go in peace.'

In the deep hours after midnight, the soothsayer woke up and quietly walked to the farmer's field in the inky darkness. After drawing water from a nearby well, he proceeded to irrigate the crops throughout the night.

'My back is nearly broken, but my reputation, at least for now, is still intact,' he consoled himself.

The next morning, the farmer was beside himself with joy.

'What a miracle!' he told his neighbours. 'It rained during the night, just like the master predicted, but only in my field.'

By now, the prophet's infallible ability to part the clouds of the present and peep into the future was known beyond the boundaries of his little town.

Then one day, an incident occurred at the royal palace that would soon require our soothsayer's services. An invaluable plate made of pure gold, one which held a lot of sentimental value for the king, went missing. The palace had been turned upside down, and every member of the royal family and the staff felt the king's wrath. Alas, no gold plate was unearthed.

The king announced a great reward to anyone who could find the missing gold plate. A wandering courtier who had heard of the soothsayer told the king of his amazing powers to foretell the future. The soothsayer was summarily summoned to calm the monarch's frayed nerves and to help find his beloved possession.

Of all the things that the lucky fortune teller had predicted, nothing about the future appeared to him as clearly as his own doom at the hands of the king. To delay being unmasked as a charlatan, he announced that he needed to first perform a grand yagna to propitiate the right deities and only then would the cosmos reveal the hiding place of the missing plate.

He asked for seclusion and a big ceremonial fire. And he then started chanting, inventing mantras from his past 'miracles'.

'Yennai chuttade dosai (Dosai pan-fried with oil). Swahaha!' he incanted as he poured ghee into the fire.

'Tedi kudithadu kazhidai (The donkey that was found). Swahaha!' he chanted.

'Yertrum iraindade tanneer (The rain brought about by the water wheel). Swahaha!' he continued.

By then, his despair combined with the smoke and heat from the fire to reduce him to sweat and tears.

'Kanni kum mooku kum gangaala pattai (The Ganga flows down from the eyes and nose). Swahaha!' he concluded.

Little did he know, but the two chambermaids who had access to the king's personal chambers were listening and peeping into the mock yagna. They had stolen the gold plate. When they heard the last incantation from the soothsayer, Kanni and Mooku (for those were their names) trembled with fear.

How had this great master divined their act of robbery?

Before a greater disaster befell them, they ran into the room, fell at the soothsayer's feet and begged before him, 'Forgive us, O Seer. We have erred. Please protect us from the king's wrath. We will bring you the gold plate immediately.'

When the soothsayer took the plate back to the king, he was elated beyond words. He kept his word and showered the soothsayer with rewards of gold and jewellery.

Once he had collected his reward, the soothsayer told his wife, 'I have tested my luck enough. It is time for us to now move to a faraway place where nobody has heard of me or my not-so-great powers.'

And so they lived happily ever after in a place that remains a secret to this day.

# Kali and the Seventh Black Pepper

Once upon a time, the king of a land had a terrible headache.

'Aiyyo, Rama! I cannot bear this. My head is going to split into a thousand pieces,' he moaned, and he groaned and wished he could have loaned his splitting head to someone else.

His vaidyar, the court doctor, told him, 'I will make you a special potion with seven black peppercorns ground into it. It will cure your headache in a jiffy.'

So he brought forth his mortar and pestle, and filled it with all kinds of spices and medicinal extracts. Then he counted seven dark-as-the-moonless-night peppercorns and sprinkled them on the other ingredients. What he didn't notice was that one of the peppercorns had rolled out of the mortar and his special potion ended up having only

six peppercorns. Blissfully unaware, the vaidyar went ahead.

He took up his pestle and made a thick ground paste of the ingredients. He added it to some tulsi water and, satisfied with the result, presented it to the king. The king, eagerly looking forward to getting rid of his headache, drank the potion in one big gulp.

'GMMMKYUMMMM!' he swallowed.

And lo! And behold! Nothing happened. You know why.

It was because of that escaped peppercorn.

Now, what happened to that escaped little spice? He went rolling along the side of the mortar, down the vaidyar's room, out of the palace and into the streets by the bazaar.

When he finally paused to take a breath, what did he see?

He saw a paati dishing up some heavenly appams, each filled with melting jaggery, ghee and bits of coconut. They were brought out of the pan, freshly deep-fried, a ripe, rich brown glistening in the sun and the oil. This was obviously Paati's secret recipe, probably handed down to her by her own grandmother years ago.

How do I know that? Because only a recipe that is so time-tested instantly makes your mouth water.

And did the peppercorn's mouth water!

The rich scent wafted through the air, tickling his taste buds, making him want to wolf down the whole basket of appams right then and there.

But Paati would have none of that.

'Don't you dare touch those appams,' she warned the peppercorn. 'If you want some for yourself, bring me the ingredients, and I will make them for you.'

So the peppercorn went off in search of the ingredients for his own batch of appams.

As he rolled down the street, he saw an empty barrel by the roadside. He rolled the barrel down to the merchant's shop, and because he was so small, nobody could see a peppercorn when he filled the barrel with jaggery and ghee and coconut and flour and oil. He then rolled it back to Paati and said, 'Here you go. Now make my own barrelful of appams.'

And so Paati whipped up the most delicious batch of appams for the peppercorn.

The peppercorn set off with his barrel of appams and settled down inside a temple of Goddess Kali. He then proceeded to chomp down on one appam after another.

'GLOMPPP GLOMPPPP!' he went. 'CHOMMMPPPP. THBKKKK. GLOMPPPP!'

It wasn't long before the scent and sight of the appams attracted Kali's attention.

She eyed the appams longingly, trying to keep her mouth from watering too much, and asked the peppercorn, 'Will you please give me one appam?'

Without diverting his attention from the appam he was gorging, the pepper absentmindedly answered, 'Yes, yes. Hold on while I eat this one.'

Kali somehow managed to control her cravings for a few more minutes, but the sight of the fast-disappearing appams was too much for her to bear.

'I hope you will leave me one appam?', she pleaded to the peppercorn.

'Haven't I already told you I will?' he snapped at her, continuing to wolf down more appams.

And before he knew it, he had wiped out the entire barrel of appams.

When Kali saw there were no more left for her, she faced the wall in a huff, turning her back to the world.

When the temple pujari arrived in the evening, he was alarmed to see the goddess facing the wall, instead of the sanctum's door. He begged her to turn around; he made all kinds of promises and entreaties, chanted many a mantra, but to no avail.

At his wits' end, he finally sent word to the king, fearing that a great misfortune might befall the land if the deity could not be convinced to turn around again.

When the king came to the temple and saw the dreaded scene for himself, he proclaimed that whoever could get Goddess Kali to do a volte face would get half his kingdom and his daughter's hand in marriage.

All manner of people came forth and tried, but no one could get Kali to budge.

By this time, the peppercorn—that same seventh black peppercorn who had escaped the king's vaidyar's mortar and pestle—woke up from his post-appam slumber and overheard what was going on.

He stepped up to the king and proclaimed that he could do what none of the others had been able to.

He sent everyone out of the temple, shut the door behind him and whispered in the goddess's ear, 'Would you like to eat some appams?'

At once, Kali turned around with a smile and agreed.

The peppercorn had achieved the impossible. The king was overjoyed but also faced a quandary. How could he give half his kingdom and his daughter to a peppercorn?

I'm sure you have guessed by now that this was no ordinary peppercorn.

As soon as the king expressed his concerns, the peppercorn turned into a handsome prince and married the princess.

And they all lived happily ever after.

## Murukku Achu

This is a hand-held device used to twist or press out different kinds of murukku and savouries to be fried. It comes with different metal discs or moulds, each with its own pattern, pressing the dough out in different shapes and sizes.

# Payasam for the Sparrow

One day, a sparrow was hopping around when he found a grain of rice: fat, bulging, glistening by itself in the sun.

He took it to the kind-looking paati, the grandmother in the house at the corner of the winding lane and asked her, 'Paati, Paati, will you please look after my grain of rice while I go brush my teeth?'

The affectionate Paati agreed without a thought.

But while she was not looking, a meandering ant chanced upon the rice grain and walked away with the burden of joy.

Sparrow returned with sparkling teeth and asked Paati for his rice grain.

'Alas,' said Paati, 'the ant seems to have taken it away when I was not looking.'

'What?' wailed Sparrow, 'How could you be so careless, Paati? Now you'll have to give me a fistful of rice for the grain you lost.'

So Paati gave him a fistful of rice.

Sparrow, although he had been so mad at Paati just a moment earlier, had not forgotten his manners.

'Thank you, Paati. Will you please look after my fistful of rice? I will just take a quick bath and be right back.'

Now, sweet old Paati couldn't refuse such a polite request, could she?

But how was she to know that as soon as Sparrow went for his bath, a beggar would turn up at her doorstep asking for alms?

So when Sparrow returned from his bath and asked for his fistful of rice, Paati had to tell him that she couldn't refuse a beggar's alms and had given that fistful of rice to him.

'What?' retorted the now apoplectic Sparrow, 'How could you do that, Paati? Now you will have to give me a whole measure of rice in place of the fistful you gave away.'

Poor Paati couldn't bear to see Sparrow's anger and promptly gave it to him. Just as quickly, Sparrow regained his cool and made another polite request of Paati.

'Paati, Paati,' he entreated, 'would you make me some payasam with this whole measure of rice that is now mine?'

'Surely,' said Paati, 'but you will have to get me the rest of the ingredients. I will need jaggery, ghee, saffron threads, cashew nuts, raisins, milk and cardamom.'

So Sparrow went to the market and bought everything. He put them in a sack and brought them back to Paati.

Paati immediately set about the task and came back to Sparrow with a steaming vessel full of delicious payasam.

'Oh, Paati, that smells divine! I can't wait to taste it.'

'Not so fast, Sparrow! It's steaming hot. Wait for a couple of minutes.'

'I can't, Paati! My mouth is watering,' said Sparrow, and dipped his beak into the hot cauldron.

'Ouch! Ooh! Aaaaaaaaaah!' Sparrow cried. 'I've burnt my tongue. This is such bad payasam. I don't want to have any of it.'

Furious, he took the cauldron of scalding hot payasam and emptied it into the nearby lake.

Now the lake, by virtue of being quite large, was also quite cool.

When Sparrow bent down to soothe his burnt mouth in its pleasant waters, he found, to his surprise, that it was also very delicious, all thanks to the sweet payasam he had emptied in it.

'Oh, this is so tasty!' he cried. 'I will drink more of it.'

Soon, Sparrow drained the whole lake. He was close to bursting. He staggered from the yard to the cowshed and, stuffing some hay into his mouth so the payasam wouldn't spill out, went to sleep.

Just then, the cow whose shed it was wandered into her home. She spotted the hay sticking out of Sparrow and pulled at it to eat it.

And then burst forth the whole lake of payasam from Sparrow. That woke Sparrow up, who flew away in alarm, yelling:

'The goats and the cows are one with the lake. As are Paati and her house, but for this, no credit shall I take.'

# The Lazy Crow

You all know how lazy Kaka the crow is, right? I'll tell you.

This happened last year.

Now, Kaka never put something away for a rainy day, whereas everyone knows that the sparrow Kurvi keeps putting things aside for such a day.

Little by little, Kurvi had collected enough grub to make a whole stash of yummy murukku, laddoo, cheedai and other sweets and savouries.

Kaka had heard of this stash. But instead of putting herself to work and making one of her own, she only put her brain to work to see how she could lay her hands on Kurvi's goodies.

One rainy day, she flew up to Kurvi's house and knocked on the door.

*The rain rages and the wind screams*
*The vanni tree's flowers shower down upon the earth,*
*From my head to my tail, the water streams*

*Friend, won't you open the door*
*and let me into your hearth?*

Now, Kurvi was not only diligent but also intelligent. She knew Kaka's sole interest was in the goodies she had stashed away. So all she said was,

*Day has just broken*
*And my kids have barely woken.*
*Let me bathe them first*
*And then see to their hunger and to their thirst.*

Kaka decided to bide her time for a while. But soon she was back. With the same song to sing.

*The rain rages and the wind screams*
*The vanni tree's flowers shower down upon the earth,*
*From my head to my tail, the water streams*
*Friend, won't you open the door and let*
*me into your hearth?*

Now, Kurvi had a lot to attend to throughout the day. She knew that, unattended, Kaka would clean out her goodie box in no time. So she simply told Kaka,

*Having broken their fast*
*I must now see to all my children,*

*From the first one to the last*
*You see, they go to the school run by Mother Hen.*

Sent away thus by Kurvi, Kaka had no option but to cower in a corner for some more time. She kept her hunger at bay by dreaming about all the goodies she would gorge on soon.

Not long after, she was back, knocking on Kurvi's door, with the same song.

*The rain rages and the wind screams*
*The vanni tree's flowers shower down upon the earth,*
*From my head to my tail, the water streams*
*Friend, won't you open the door and let*
*me into your hearth?*

By now, Kurvi had sent her kids off to Mother Hen's school with umbrellas that matched their uniforms. A soggy sun had already curved its way across half the sky to the other side of the day. So she told Kaka,

*I have so much to do*
*And so little day.*
*It's been hours since cock-a-doodle doo,*

*Will you come back once I've*
*done some more, pray?*

By the time Kaka came back a fourth time, night had fallen.

Kurvi had tucked her little ones into bed when Kaka came knocking again, with her now familiar song.

*The rain rages and the wind screams*
*The vanni tree's flowers shower down upon the earth,*
*From my head to my tail, the water streamsFriend,*
*won't you open the door and let me*
*into your hearth?*

Kurvi thought,

*It's night, way past twilight*
*No harm in letting her in just for shelter.*
*My goodies are all packed and sealed tight,*
*Who knows, she might have turned a new leaf*
*for the better.*

So saying, Kurvi let Kaka into the guest room and went to bed herself. After a little while, Kurvi was woken up by what suspiciously sounded like crunching sounds, as if someone was munching away on some murukku.

'What is that noise, Kaka?' she called out, still tucked in her bed.

'What noise?' said Kaka, pretending not to know anything about it.

'Then it must be my imagination,' said Kurvi and went back to sleep.

But after a little while, she was woken up by the sound again. 'There!' she said, 'I distinctly heard it this time.'

'It's nothing,' responded Kaka. 'I had brought back some whole betel nuts from my village. I'm just taking a crack at them. I will try to be quieter with it.'

Satisfied with this answer, Kurvi went back to sleep.

Kaka, meanwhile, made the most of the opportunity and cleaned out the goodie box, down to the last murukku crumb, laddoo pearl and cheedai.

Soon, she was groaning in pain, her stomach nearly bursting.

Still perched on the goodie box, she could only relieve herself the way nature intended. So lazy, gluttony, mean old Kaka did kakka right there—in the now-empty goodie container! She closed the lid on it and, without waiting for morning to come knocking, let herself out and flew away.

The next morning was a Sunday. Kurvi's little ones woke up late and demanded a treat as soon as they jumped out of their beds. When Kurvi brought out the goodie box and opened it, all she found was Kaka's kakka. The crafty crow had left behind no trace of her murukku, cheedai or laddoo!

Kurvi figured out what had happened in the night. Without shedding a tear, she rustled up some snacks for her kids and went about her days as before. Over the course of the winter and then spring, and summer, she once again put aside little titbits from time to time and soon had a full goodie box again.

When the rains came back a year later, who should come back to knock at Kurvi's door but shameless old Kaka! You'll remember her song.

*The rain rages and the wind screams*
*The vanni tree's flowers shower down upon the earth,*
*From my head to my tail, the water streams*
*Friend, won't you open the door and let*
*me into your hearth?*

To Kaka's surprise, the door opened at once, and there was Kurvi with a welcoming smile.

*Of course, Friend, come right in.*
*Better than out will be if you spend the night in.*
*I will prepare you a nice, warm bath.*
*That will relieve you from nature's fury and wrath.*

She ushered Kaka into the bath, and as Kaka settled into the tub, Kurvi brought along two steaming buckets of scalding hot water and poured them inside.

Squealing out in agony, Kaka hopped out of the bath and flew right out of the house, chastened with a lesson that she would not forget in a hurry. And Kurvi and her little ones lived happily ever after.

## Vilakku

A traditional oil lamp usually made of brass or bronze, it's central to daily prayer rituals and is lit at the start of the day and at dusk.

# The Monkey and the Drum

*There was a monkey whose tail*
*Got stuck in a thorn.*
*He let out a long wail*
*Before he decided to grab the*
*bull by the horns.*

*He hailed a passing barber to come to his rescue*
*And the barber whipped out his shaving knife.*
*But alas, his hand slipped, and because of the miscue*
*There started a whole chain of strife.*

*Oh, you miserable* barberian,
*Look what you've done!*
*Exclaimed the newly tail-less simian.*
*'Only a while ago I had one tail,*
*and now I have none.'*
*'It looks like my bottom was bitten by an alligator,*

*And nobody is going to give me a tail on lease.*
*Your knife in exchange for my posterior elongator,*
*And right now, if you please.'*

*Anon, across the path of the round-bottomed ape*
*Came a man biting his teeth into a mango.*
*Before the man's eyes widened and*
*his mouth went agape,*
*The monkey proposed that his knife and the mango*
*do a tango.*

*Alas, the skin of the fruit was like leather*
*And instead of the man's teeth, the razor broke.*
*At this, the monkey's temper erupted like bad weather*
*Into a whole lot of fire and some smoke.*

*'You have poor excuse for teeth,*
*And you're a poorer excuse of a man.*
*I cannot even, now, put this knife back into its sheath*
*Pay me back with that mango, and quick,*
*you orangutan!'*

*And so onwards wandered*
*this bare-buttocked baboon's cousin*

*Soon, he met a hungry man with a mound*
*of cooked rice to eat.*
*Now, he may not have had cashews*
*to garnish it, or the odd raisin,*
*But our Ancestor of Pithecanthropus*
*did have one mango, sweet.*

*In one big gulp, our gullible guy with the grain*
*Made light work of the mango (minus the seed),*
*Only to see the monkey*
*(minus a tail plus a feeble brain).*
*You can guess what the monkey demanded*
*from him in greed.*

*'My mango, my magnificent mango!*
*You gobbling glutton!*
*For this impertinence, you shall pay full price.*
*Were it that I had sewn up your mouth,*
*and sealed it with a button*
*But the damage is done, and for that,*
*you will give me all your rice.'*

*It might seem like this story has been written*
*Only to show you how easy it is to get*

*the monkey up to a boil.*
*But read on, dear reader, and perhaps*
*you shall also be smitten*
*By the same illness that befell—on sighting our*
*monkey—this seller of oil.*

*'You seem like you haven't eaten in days,*
*Why don't you partake of this rice? It is well-cooked.'*
*The oil seller thought,*
*'He seems to mean what he says.'*
*Oh, if only the peddler of*
*frying fat hadn't gone on about how he looked.*

*And so, it was only a matter of time*
*Before this bandar from somewhere*
*(not Down Under).*
*Exploded like a ball of gob and slime*
*All the oil seller could do was fold his*
*arms in meek surrender.*
*'For eating up all my rice, you shall pay the price,'*
*Thundered the lamer-than-a-lemur monkey*
*without a wagger.*
*'Give me all your oil, and give it to me in a trice.'*

*You'd think for someone with no tail, he wouldn't*
*have such swagger.*
*Well, by now you know the entire drill.*
*Down the road from the oil seller, there was a dosa-*
*making paati*
*Who should get a whiff of the frying dosas but our*
*copy-cat mandrill.*
*What he saw, though, made him sad, not naughty.*

*The adorable paati had no oil to make the dosa*
*'Here, Paati,' said our suddenly generous macaque,*
*'Take this oil, for without it, a dosa would be worse*
*than a samosa.'*
*Paati gratefully took the oil before*
*he could take it back.*

*But now that the oil had been used up*
*The monkey set up his familiar lament.*
*'I see your dosas are all nicely spruced up,*
*But all I have left of the*
*oil is this can as an ornament.'*
*'Paati, not for a minute does*
*your cunning deceive me*

*You'd better give me all your dosas*
*immediately, or else ...'*
*'No, no,' exclaimed Paati, aghast.*
*'This isn't how I'd like you to see me.*
*Don't you believe I'm cunning, regardless*
*of what, to you, anybody tells.'*

*Just as the dosa-laden monkey*
*reached the village temple, it started to rain.*
*There, in a corner, sat the percussion*
*maestro with his big fat drum.*
*And the monkey once again listened not to his*
*stomach but to his monkey brain*
*'O Melakaar, you look hungry, as if inside you, your*
*stomach is causing mayhem.'*

*'Would you like some dosas to quell that infernal*
*internal intestinal kutcheri?'*
*Asked the suddenly solicitous son of a capuchin.*
*'Now, there,' thought the drummer,*
*'is a cake with a cherry*
*If ever I saw one,' eyeing the bulging box,*
*the sizzling dosas were in.*

*Recklessly, like all those preceding him,*
*he wolfed it all down*
*This, of course, was guaranteed*
*to get the monkey's goat.*
*'How dare you gobble up my dosas,'*
*yelled the monkey, 'each so crisp and brown?*
*'What cheek you have to do that*
*while not a morsel has gone*
*down my throat!'*

*The drummer was caught between*
*the heavenly satisfaction*
*Having just enjoyed a dozen dosas, really well-made.*
*And the imitation tamarin's somewhat*
*righteous indignation*
*On the whole, he thought*
*the dosas for a monkey's anger*
*were a good trade.*

*The monkey, though, wasn't feeling as charitable*
*'Hand over your melam, you devourer*
*of my dosas divine.*
*'I am never going to invite you to*

*eat again at my table.'*
*The relieved drummer thought,*
*'If that is all I have to do, then I am fine.'*

*The monkey jumped onto the temple wall*
*With the drum in his hands.*
*He addressed all assembled in the temple hall,*
*And the multitudes, beyond,*
*in the many stands.*

*'I lost my tail but gained a knife,* dum-dum-dum!
*I lost a knife but gained a mango,* dum-dum-dum!
*I lost a mango but gained some rice,* dum-dum-dum!
*I lost the rice but gained some oil,* dum-dum-dum!

*I lost the oil but gained some*
*dosas,* dum-dum-dum!
*I lost the dosas but gained a melam,*
dum-dum-dum!'

*So saying, he threw the drum*
*into the temple tank*
*The water of the tank he then drank.*

*You see now, don't you, that however*
*much you try to train,*
*That is all there is to a monkey brain!*

# The Newly Rich Sparrow

*Once upon a time, there was*
*a proud little sparrow*
*Who found himself a paisa, new and shiny.*
*He flew fast and straight as an arrow*
*To the king's huge palace, even though he himself*
*was so tiny.*

*In his head, he morphed into a larger bird*
*Crowing for all he was worth*
*about his new-found wealth.*
*He sat atop the king's palace to spread his word*
*'I am the owner of a shiny new paisa,*
*by chance and not by stealth!'*

*Over and over at the top of his voice,*
*this mantra he repeated*
*As if he had more riches than anyone*
*else in the world.*
*The king, who thought himself the richest, and did*

*not like this way to be treated*
*When he heard this, he considered it*
*an insult at him, hurled.*

*'Snatch the paisa from that braggart,'*
*he commanded his guard*
*'The bird's louder and prouder*
*than a peacock with his fan.'*
*'And while it may not be much,'*
*he instructed the court bard*
*'Compose a poem for this occasion that will forever*
*live with my clan.'*

*The miffed sparrow–crow–peacock was not one to*
*yield so easily*
*To be deprived thus of his wordly gains.*
*'He isn't just a poor loser, he's*
*poor too,' he chanted breezily,*
*'This pauper disguised as a king, for just a single*
*paisa, going to such pains.'*

*The taunt hit home, and the king ordered*
*the paisa to be returned*

*But, alas, that only encouraged the*
*cocky sparrow more!*
*He figured this was a good chance for the king's*
*temper to be churned*
*He clutched the paisa in a claw as he took wing,*
*intent to be part of folklore.*

*'Loser, pauper, scaredy-cat,'*
*He sang, soaring safely out of reach*
*of the king's hand.*
*'That's not a crown on his head,*
*more a mad hatter's hat.'*
*So saying, he took himself and his*
*paisa to a distant land.*

## Veshti

A wraparound lower-body garment worn by men, made of cotton or silk. It is traditionally white in colour, with an embroidered or coloured border that can be a simple strip or ornate with gold work.

# Athiripaacha

Before I forget, I must remember to tell you the first thing you must know about Malini's husband: he was very forgetful.

One day, Madhusudhan woke up and started remembering all the good times he had had with his friend, Murali, when they were young boys.

Now, the very act of remembering was a miracle for a forgetful man like Madhu, thought his wife Malini.

'Listen,' she said, 'if you like Murali so much that you can remember him, then you must go and meet him before you forget about him altogether.'

'That's an excellent idea! I think I will go tomorrow itself,' agreed Madhu.

Murali lived in a distant village, so Madhu decided to start early the next morning.

When he got to his friend's home, Madhu found that Murali, too, had similar, joyous memories of their youth. Together, they regaled themselves with

# Kozhakattai Recipe

stories of the past and then brought themselves up to speed with their lives in the present day.

Murali's wife, Meera, meanwhile, whipped up some steaming fresh kozhakattais. What are kozhakattais, you ask?

Let me tell you.

You know what an idli is, right? Well, think of this as a super-delicious, better-than-idli dish made in an idli steamer. It's made of broken rice, it's got yummy coconut pieces in it and you can even ask Amma to put in a few cashew nuts. And I'm sure Amma knows how to fry the whole red chilli just enough for its taste to seep into every single kozhakattai, even though you will never bite into a piece of red chilli ever. And, of course, when the kozhakattai comes out of the steamer, it's nice and plump and oval, like a chubby-cheeked egg, but way yummier.

When Madhu tasted Meera's kozhakattais, he couldn't stop eating them. He had never had such a preparation before, and he found them so good that he devoured the whole batch and lost himself in the layered taste of this newly discovered delight.

At the end of his visit, Madhu left Murali and Meera's home with a happy tummy and a supremely satisfied set of taste buds.

He resolved to tell Malini about the magical kozhakattais and thought of asking her to make some regularly. So as not to forget about it, he kept chanting the name all along the way back.

'Kozhakattai, kozhakattai, kozhakattai ...' he went as he wended his way back home.

He passed village and vale, forest and field, and passers-by could see a fleeting figure intensely chanting something to himself.

'What a devout man,' they thought to themselves.

'Kozhakattai, kozhakattai, kozhakattai ...' chanted Madhu, without pausing. Halfway into his journey, Madhu halted in a grove to refresh himself. To get respite from the midday sun, he found a large banyan tree under which a group of people were already enjoying the cool shade. He sat at a small distance from the lot, with his back to them, leaning against the broad girth of the banyan tree.

The men in the group, it seemed, were discussing a recent incident in their village involving one of their neighbours whose name was Athiripaacha.

For the next half hour, all Madhu could hear was Athiripaacha this, Athiripaacha that.

'Did you hear what Athiripaacha did?' one man animatedly asked.

'And that's not the half of it. Athiripaacha …' continued another.

'Athiripaacha then went on to …'

'Athiripaacha did what? How could he?'

'You have to hand it to Athiripaacha. That was very bold of him.'

'Bold? And Athiripaacha? Harrumph! That's nothing.'

And on the conversation went. Madhu was slowly being lulled into a pleasant sleep by the hum of their voices and the afternoon sun filtering in through the banyan tree's leafy branches. When he awoke, he found himself alone; the group of men had left while he was asleep. Picking up his belongings, Madhu continued his journey. After a few steps, he remembered to resume his chant so he could tell Malini what to cook for him when he got home.

His forgetful brain helpfully offered what it had most recently heard. And so, try as he might, the word that Madhu was able to summon up to chant was, you guessed it, Athiripaacha!

And so he walked, resuming his uninterruptible chant.

'Athiripaacha, athirpaacha, athiripaacha ...' he chanted as he crossed stream and street.

When he reached home, the first words Malini heard when she opened the door for him were 'Athiripaacha, athiripaacha, athiripaacha.'

Naturally curious, she asked him what he was going on about.

So Madhu told her that Athiripaacha was the name of perhaps the most delicious dish he had ever had.

'Athiripaacha? I've never heard of a dish called Athiripaacha!' said a surprised Malini.

'What do you mean you've never heard of it? It's the best thing I've ever eaten. I'm sure it's a really famous dish. How can you possibly not even know of it?'

'Well, that's such a strange name for food. Athiripaacha! Whoever has heard of such a thing?

It doesn't sound like the name of a dish at all,' went Malini.

That only riled Madhu even more.

'I'm telling you that was the name of the dish. I chanted the name all along my way back just so I would remember to tell you to make it for me. I'm not making it up.'

'Well, all I can tell you is that I've never heard of it. And if I don't know what it is, how can I make it for you?' responded Malini.

This only made Madhu madder, and his pale face bulged in rage. Hearing his raised voice, the neighbours rushed in and tried to check on them.

'What is wrong? Why are you berating the poor woman?' they asked. 'And look at your angry face, it's all swollen and become plump like a kozhakattai.'

'Kozhakattai! That's it! That was the name of the dish I had eaten. Maalu, that's what I was trying to tell you,' exclaimed a beaming Madhu.

The neighbours and Malini didn't know whether to laugh or to cry. In the end, Malini made a big batch of kozhakattais for everyone, and they lived happily ever after.

# Mother Hen's Grain

By the pond at the corner of the village where the woods began, there once lived Mother Hen with her little brood of cheeping chicks.

One morning, Mother Hen came out of her roost with a big basket of grain. She was in a generous mood and decided she would share them with her neighbours.

'I've got a big basket of grain here. Who will come around and help me separate the grain from the chaff? Who will come around? Is there anyone who will come around to separate the grain from the chaff?' she called out.

'Not I,' said the crow, pretending to be too busy preening himself to be able to help.

'Not I,' said the sparrow, bustling about here and there, while keeping an eye out for a few loose grains to fall from the basket so she could keep them for herself.

'Not I,' said the parrot, too lazy to want to

work for his food, pecking at yesterday's half-eaten mango instead.

'Not I,' said the duck, waddling away a little farther from the bank before she could be roped in.

So Mother Hen set about all by herself, carefully threshing the grain to separate it from the chaff. Once she was done, she thought she would give her neighbours another chance to partake of her harvest by helping out with the next step.

'I've separated the grain from the chaff. Now, who will come around to help me pound the grain into flour? Who will come around? Is there anyone who will come around to pound the grain into flour?' she called.

'Not I,' said the crow, gargling water down his long black throat as his morning ablutions were too important to be interrupted.

'Not I,' said the sparrow, not yet having laid hands on any grain but not wanting to work for her food either.

'Not I,' said the parrot, even though he found that yesterday's mango had become home to two worms today.

'Not I,' said the duck, although she could spot no fish to fish for her meals either.

So Mother Hen set about pounding the grain into flour all by herself. Once she was done, she thought she would give her neighbours yet another chance to partake of her harvest by helping out with the next step.

'I've pounded the grain into flour. Now, who will come around to help me sift the flour to mix and knead? Who will come around? Is there anyone who will come around to sift the flour to mix and knead?' she called.

'Not I,' said the crow, 'I don't want to taint my black feathers with that powdery white flour.'

'Not I,' said the sparrow, starting to feel hungry but still not desperate enough to want to participate in sifting.

'Not I,' said the parrot, thinking that if Mother Hen was going to do everything by herself, he might as well wait for her to prepare the food.

'Not I,' said the duck, 'my webbed feet won't help your cause.'

So Mother Hen set about sifting the flour to knead and mix it all by herself. Once she was done, she thought she would give her neighbours one last chance to partake of her harvest by helping out with the next step.

'I've sifted the grain to knead and mix. Now, who will come around to help me turn the kneaded flour into hot chapatis? Who will come around? Is there anyone who will come around to turn the kneaded flour into hot chapatis?' she called.

'Not I,' said the crow, delighted that he was only one step away from enjoying Mother Hen's hot chapatis.

'Not I,' said the sparrow, for once thinking like a crow.

'Not I,' said the parrot, in the same boat.

'Not I,' said the duck, 'the dough will get stuck in my bill.'

So Mother Hen set about making hot chapatis from the kneaded dough all by herself. Once she was done, she called out to her neighbours again.

'I've made hot chapatis from the kneaded dough. Now, who will come around to eat them? Who will come around? Is there anyone who will come around to eat the hot chapatis?' she called.

‘I will!’ cried the crow, barely able to stop himself from drooling.

‘I will!’ said the sparrow, excited but trying not to sound too greedy.

‘I will!’ said the parrot, forgetting all his naysaying until then.

‘I will!’ said the duck, her webbed feet no longer a problem.

*‘Aasa dosai appalam vadai!’* replied Mother Hen. ‘Like I will give you any piece of the chapatis now. You were too lazy to do any of the work and made me do all of it, and now you want to line up to eat? I’m not giving you a single bite,’ she said.

And taking her heap of hot chapatis, she went back to her brood in her roost and fed them all the fluffy hot chapatis.

## Kolam

A daily ritual in most Tamil households where the threshold of the house is cleaned every morning and adorned with a decorative design hand-drawn using rice flour. The Kolam also serves as food for small insects and birds and is a way of giving back to nature.

# The Chicken's Heavenward Journey

'Listen,' said Appa to me, taking over the mantle of storytelling from Amma for a change. And this is the story he sang.

*There once was a chicken*
*Who was about to be eaten.*
*Since there was some time before he reached heaven*
*He decided to enjoy himself until then.*

*He made a song and dance of his situation*
*And saw it as a chance for some laughter.*
*He put words into a musical formation*
*And become an immortal legend forever after.*

'Tandaana tandaana!' *he sang.*
*'Here comes the knife that will undress me.*
*I'm going to get a shave and a haircut while I'm at it.*
'Tandaana tandaana!' *he sang.*
'Tandaana tandaana!' *he sang.*

*'Here comes the water that will wash me.*
*'I'm going to cleanse myself in the holy Ganga*
*while I'm at it.*
'Tandaana tandaana!' *he sang.*

'Tandaana tandaana!' *he sang.*
*'Here comes a hot water-filled pot in*
*which I will stew.*
Taa tai, takka tai, *I'm going to dance*
*merrily while I'm at it.*
'Tandaana tandaana!' *he sang.*

'Tandaana tandaana!' *he sang.*
*'Here comes a mouth that will swallow me.*
*Oh, I'm heading heavenwards, ta-ta bye-bye!*
'Tandaana tandaana!' *he sang.*

'And that's how,' Appa concluded, 'the wise little chicken taught me that even if life lands you in hot water, you can jump and dance and make light of the situation until it passes!'

# The Tortoise and the Fly

Once upon a time in a gurukulam, there lived two young students.

Minnal, like the Tamil word for 'lightning' he was named after, was a bright spark and very quick to answer any questions their guru posed.

On the other hand, Aamai, as his name suggests, was slow to get off the mark. Oh, and just in case you thought that was his real name, it was not. His parents didn't name him after a tortoise. The nickname was given to him in the gurukulam because, on some counts, Aamai wasn't the quickest off the blocks.

Aamai was tireless when it came to walking in the forest that surrounded the gurukulam, while all the other students would tire themselves out quickly.

But when it came to his studies, Aamai truly lived up to his name. It was as if his guru's teachings would reach his eyes and ears, and then the words found it too difficult to cover the distance from his sense organs to his brain. In reality, his brain had no problem quickly processing things his eyes saw and his ears heard. It just preferred to use all its powers to think of the cool pond Aamai had discovered on one of his forest walks. Or savour the juicy mangoes that hung liltingly out of his reach on the branches. Or the perfect Y-shaped stick he saw with which to make a catapult.

Panini's grammar was lost on Aamai. As for Brahmagupta's and Aryabhatta's greatest contribution to the world of mathematics, it was all a big zero for Aamai.

'Aamai, how much is eleven multiplied by eleven?' his guru asked him once.

Aamai scratched his hair, tried to unblock his ears, blinked a few times and even looked skywards.

When no answer was forthcoming from the heavens, Aamai heaved a sigh and summoned up a solution from somewhere in the recesses of his brain.

'Eleventy-eleven!' he proclaimed.

The whole class—including his guru—burst out laughing, some of his peers even rolling on the floor.

'My dear Aamai, I don't think we are all ready yet for your advanced level of mathematics,' the guru said while wiping tears of laughter.

Another time, the guru wanted to test his students' knowledge of animals. He posed the following riddle.

'What is that animal that moves around but never changes its spots?'

Like a flash, Minnal's hand shot up, and he answered, 'A leopard!'

The guru beamed at Minnal, proud of his knowledge and his quick-wittedness.

He turned to Aamai and asked him the next question—a much simpler one.

'What is the creature that sounds the wake-up call every morning to announce the sun's arrival?' he asked.

Poor Aamai's brain refused to wake up sufficiently to answer the question. 'I wish that wretched creature were here to wake me up right now,' he thought to himself.

Once again, something stirred somewhere deep in his brain.

'A dog barks in the morning, but the answer is not a dog, I know that much,' he pondered.

'It's not these hens either, cackling away all the time,' he reasoned in his head. 'Oh, Aamai, you're so close. Wrack your brain! You can do it! Your brain only needs a small booster.'

Putting two and two together, the dog and the booster became one, and Aamai triumphantly answered, 'Dooster!'

'Ha ha ha ha, Aamai! You have outdone yourself this time,' cried the guru with laughter. 'I have heard of the makara, an aquatic creature with the features of a deer, a crocodile, an elephant and a fish. I have heard of the kimara, half-bird and half-human. I have heard of the sharabha, a part-lion, part-bird with eight legs. But I have never heard of a "dooster" before until now!'

It was such incidents that showed how far and wide Aamai's knowledge and imagination could travel. Now you may think, 'What kind of a guru is this who did not mind if his student gave such wild, imaginative answers? Didn't they have to pass any examinations in the gurukulam?'

That's a very good question, and it's exactly why the guru summoned Aamai to talk to him.

'Listen to me carefully, Aamai,' the guru said. 'You know that before you can graduate from the gurukulam, you have to pass the final examination.'

'Yes, master,' answered Aamai calmly, although deep inside he was all aflutter, wondering how on earth he would pass the exam.

'If you have learnt anything here,' the guru continued, 'I hope it is this: I don't need my students to know everything. But they must know how to learn about everything. Do you see the difference?'

Aamai only vaguely understood what the guru was saying.

'Let me explain further,' the guru explained. 'In the final exam, there will be questions from every field of knowledge.'

'Even astr ... astr ... astronomy, master?' muttered Aamai. For if there was one subject that made Aamai see stars even in the day, it was astronomy.

'Yes, Aamai, even astronomy. But don't worry. Like I said, you don't have to know everything about every subject to pass the gurukulam's exam. You will be sitting next to Minnal. All I want you to do is copy whatever he is writing in his parchment. Do you understand? Minnal will know all the answers. And by replicating his words, you will have the opportunity to know all the answers from him. Remember, all you have to do is copy him exactly. Copy. Him. Exactly.'

Aamai was as thrilled as he was relieved to hear this. He was now sure of graduating from the gurukulam. After all, Minnal wouldn't fail the final exam. how could Aamai fail? And so when the day of the final exam arrived, Aamai was as confident as, if not more so than, Minnal.

The students all took their seats, Minnal sitting next to Aamai.

The guru would ask one question at a time, allowing the students to write their answers on their palm leaves.

'If a crow flies east for 8 kilometres, then north for 9 kilometres, then west for 7 kilometres and finally south for 11 kilometres, how far is it from where it started?'

Minnal quickly put quill to leaf and furiously started writing out his answer. Next to him, Aamai showed he was no slow coach when it came to the speed of his quill, copying Minnal.

'Why don't lions and tigers live in the same jungles?' came the guru's next question.

Aamai thanked his stars—and his guru—for being able to copy Minnal's answer. Left to his devices, he would never have known that tigers are solitary creatures that hunt with stealth through dense forests, while lions hunt in packs in open grasslands.

He saw Minnal write this and faithfully copied the answer, word for word.

'What kind of a poet is a vikata-kavi?' the guru asked next.

'Aamai, did you know if you read the syllables backwards, it still spells vi-ka-ta-ka-vi?' asked Minnal, while writing about jester poets, the most famous of them being Tenali Raman.

At this point, just as Aamai was busy replicating Minnal's answer onto his palm leaf, a fly landed on Minnal's palm leaf.

With a swift thwack, Minnal swatted the fly, turning it into a watermark on the palm leaf.

Aamai saw what Minnal had just done and frantically looked about. There was no fly on his palm leaf. There was no fly anywhere near him. Or near Minnal.

Desperately, he looked around the room for a fly. The guru had told him he must do exactly what Minnal did. That meant 'ee adicha copy'—if he hits a fly, copy him!

But where was he going to find a fly to swat on his palm leaf? And then he spotted one. There it was, buzzing just above his guru's head.

Gleefully, Aamai made a beeline for his guru's head, his palm leaf in one hand and the other ready to swat the fly onto it.

The guru was about to start his next question when he saw Aamai sprinting towards him, hands outstretched as if to slap both his ears.

Thwack!

Aamai's empty hand met his palm leaf. But alas! The fly flew away just in time.

It went and settled on Minnal's head. This time, Aamai promptly dashed towards him.

By then, the whole gurukulam was doubled over, laughing at Aamai's race around the courtyard, chasing the fly from one head to another. Clearly, this tortoise would have beaten any hare in any race, given the speed at which he was racing around.

'Stop, Aamai, stop!' cried the guru. 'Never mind the fly. I now declare that you have passed the exam with flying colours. It's clear that you are clearly seeing—and learning from—every single thing Minnal is doing.'

Aamai beamed. He had passed the final exam. He was not so slow after all!

## Vengalapaanai

A heavy, round pot typically made of bronze and used to cook rice or pongal.

# Kokku, the Side-Blinded Crane

I'm sure you've seen horses on the street at some point. You know how they wear patches on the sides of their eyes, so they are always focused only on the road in front of them? That way, they are not distracted by anything else around them, to the left or to the right.

Those patches are called side blinders, and now you know about side-blinded horses (if you didn't know about them before).

But have you ever heard of a side-blinded crane? I guessed as much.

Let me tell you about Kokku, the side-blinded crane.

Kokku, like all birds of his species, would fly far and wide every day, from one pond to another in search of food. Now, there's nothing fishy about this when I tell you that meen—I mean, fish—were his favourite food.

One particular day, Kokku found a new pond. As he was swooping down from the sky, he spotted a lot of fish darting around the water.

He spotted some goldfish, glinting in the sun. He also saw some guppies, very plain-looking. He didn't care for either of them.

'Huh! Goldfish are the peacocks of the pond. Pretty but pretty useless. And pretty tasteless too, I must add,' he harrumphed out loud to nobody in particular.

And then his eyes lit up.

Because he had seen a big school of mrigal and virameen and jilabee. And in between them all, the most delicious of all, the ayirai—small, spiny and yummy (to Kokku, at least).

Now, the meen—all varieties of them—were no slow-moving aamai (tortoise). As soon as Kokku's descending shadow started to fall on the surface, they scurried away in all directions.

Some went hither and some went thither. The mrigal merged with the weeds. The jilabee squiggled away, its fast-moving body drawing dizzying shapes in the water.

Kokku tried to dart in all directions as fast as the fish were scattering, but not one fish came into his grasp. And then, he got lucky.

Right under a shallow spot in the pond where he was standing, a shoal of ayirai plunged into a hollow cavity in the pond bed.

Alas, it turned out to be a dead end, with no way out except to be airlifted into Kokku's gullet!

GULP!! GOBBLE!!! GMMMYUKKK!!!

Kokku swallowed large mouthfuls of ayirai, hardly able to believe his luck. He had so many that day, he could hardly take wing afterwards to get back to his home.

Later that night, Kokku relived his lucky day.

'So. Many. Ayirai. Each was tastier than the one before. Burp! Even the aftertaste was delicious! Oh, how they swam right under my feet and into the hollow I was standing in!' he reminisced.

'The hollow! That's why I got so lucky. Because they couldn't go anywhere once they entered it. Oooooh! All I need to do from now on is fly to that pond and wait in the hollow. Tra la la! My unlucky days are so over!'

The more he thought about it, the happier he got.

And then he remembered another detail. He had lifted one leg as a stream of ayirai swam into the hollow.

'That's my lucky pose from now on. Why use both legs when I can stand perfectly on one? More room for more of the helpless ayirai to swim into the hollow!'

Dreaming of an endless supply of fish for the rest of his days, Kokku dozed off into a happy slumber.

He woke up later than usual the next morning.

'Huh! I'm not a lowly worm-eater that I have to rise and be an early bird. I have the Ayirai Tank all to myself.'

So saying he preened himself at leisure. When the sun was a quarter of the way across the sky, Kokku finally ascended skywards. He flew straight to the Ayirai Kolam—the Ayirai Tank—as he now called it.

Straight as an arrow, he flew to the spot directly above the hollow in the water and descended like a helicopter, hovering right there and gently placing one leg into the water.

He bowed his head towards the water and balanced himself perfectly on one leg. And there he stood. Not in vrikshasana—the yogic tree pose—because that would mean he would gaze out to the horizon. If he stood in vrikshasana, how could he keep an eye out for ayirai? So, no, Kokku was not standing in vrikhasana.

Instead, he assumed the eka pada tadasana—the one-legged mountain pose. No, silly, you and I both know that mountains don't have legs, not even one. Stop getting distracted. Can you see Kokku now? There he is. In the middle of the pond. With one leg raised skywards. The other leg planted firmly, through the water, on the hollow shelf in the pond bed. His head facing downwards, his eyes locked straight into the water. He looks like an upside-down Y standing there, doesn't he?

All around him, the fish in the pond went about their business. The guppies are blowing kisses to the weeds. The goldfish are preening each other. The jilabee is teasing the mrigal, swimming squiggly circles around them.

But where are the ayirai? Now, the ayirai may have been the smallest fish in the pond. But they were certainly not stupid. They had seen what had happened to their friends yesterday, becoming Kokku's breakfast, lunch and dinner.

And so today, they steadfastly avoided the hollow.

Kokku, meanwhile, stood steadfast. He was not going to be distracted by anything, he vowed.

Virameen streaked past him on the left. Guppies to his right. The mrigal is a foot from his nose. And still Kokku stood there, unmoving.

Just then, a flock of cranes flying over the pond saw this strange sight of Kokku in eka pada tadasana. They flew down to the pond.

'What are you doing in this pose, Kokku?' one of them asked him.

'Can't you see? This pond is full of yummy fish,' he replied.

'We can see that,' his friend replied. 'But why are you standing like this? Why aren't you trying to catch them?'

'Oh, you foolish crane,' Kokku replied, 'in this pond, I don't have to go after the fish to catch them. They come straight to me. Watch and learn from a master.'

The other cranes stood (on both legs) and watched Kokku. Fish swam all around him, but none of them were accepting Kokku's imaginary invitation to be swallowed by him.

Seeing all the fish in the pond, though, the other cranes got busy chasing them, trying to catch them as they darted about.

As for Kokku, he continued to stand with his unwavering gaze fixed on the hollow under the water.

'Kokku, we've eaten our fill from this pond. We're going to leave now. Don't you want to try and catch some fish too?' the other cranes suggested.

'Go away! You're scaring away my precious ayirai from coming to me,' Kokku snapped at them.

Realising there was no point arguing with Kokku, the cranes flew away. As if on cue, the skies opened up suddenly, and a huge downpour began.

Kokku remained unflappable.

Drenched but unperturbed, he kept his eye on the hollow, his bottom pointing to the sky.

A little later, the rain stopped, and the sun started burning bright as if to make up for lost time. But that didn't deter Kokku one bit either.

There he stood for hours, while the fish now came within a few inches of his beak, sure he would not move an inch to the left or right.

Soon, the sun was tired and started sinking into the horizon. The flock of cranes, on their way back home, peered down at the pond.

And there, still, stood Kokku.

Legend has it that if you go to Ayirai Kolam even today, you'll find Kokku still standing there in eka pada tadasana. He still hasn't caught a single fish. But he wears his side-blinders. And he still believes that the ayirai will come to him on their own.

# Eli, the Rat Who Got Fat in the Pot That Was Hot

*Once upon a time, there lived a rat.*
*His name was Eli, and he was so, so, so thin*
*That you could mistake him for a gnat.*
*Like a gnat, he tried to fly, tucking his tail in*
*But all he managed was a big, fat splat!*

*He nibbled on some green, green grass.*
*'Eww!' he went, 'that's so gross!'*
*He bit into a chunk of shiny, shiny glass.*
*'My teeth will show this glass who's boss!'*
*With a broken tooth after, he said, 'The glass might as well have been brass.'*

*'Oooh!' he cried out. 'That looks like a juicy, juicy piece of wood!'*
*In addition to being hungry, he was also just so, so eager.*

*'I bet that tastes very, very, very good.'*
*Alas, he was just a rat, not at all a beaver.*
*Biting off less than he could chew,*
*that much he understood.*

*'What's that over there? It looks soft and orangey.'*
*Eli had spotted Paati's narthangai—salty,*
*sweet lime rinds.*
*Not yet dry in the sun, they certainly were spongy.*
*Elit bit into it and caught himself in two minds.*
*The narthangai, he discovered, was*
*neither soft nor crunchy.*

*He found his way into Paati's larder.*
*What should he spot next but Paati's special mango*
*pickle: avakkai*
*He bit into it and shot up! Oh, not on a ladder.*
*The fiery red chilli and sour mango sent*
*him into the sky.*
*This only made Eli hungrier and madder.*

*And then his eyes lit up upon spotting*
*ants making a beeline.*

*'Wait a minute,' he thought. 'Do bees*
*make an ant line?*
*'I know cows are bovine and cats are feline.'*
*His stomach growled, reminding him again that his*
*hunger was elephantine.*
*And so, he, too went to the pot of honey, like the ants,*
*made a beeline.*

*'Ooh! Eww!! Icky!!! Sticky!!!!'*
*He couldn't understand why ants loved the honey*
*'I'll eat pretty much anything, I'm not very picky.*
*But honey, I couldn't eat it even*
*if you gave me money.*
*How am I going to make myself un-sticky?*
*This is tricky!'*

*Just then, he spotted a crow outside the window.*
*He (the crow) had come for a kaka kuli—a bird bath.*
*Eli saw it and said, 'Getting myself*
*un-sticky—that's how!'*
*He looked up and did some mental math.*
*In three bounds, he was in the*
*bath and back again below.*
*Something was gnawing away*

*inside him all this while.*
*He realised, again, that it was his starving stomach.*
*It was now frowning in anger, sporting an upside-down smile.*
*He needed food, and for right now, he needed luck.*
*He wondered, 'Why can't I spot any food?*
*Am I growing senile?'*
*And then, he smelt it from a distance.*
*Ghee, rice, pepper and cashews in a heady mix.*
*His favourite delicious pongal,*
*he could tell at a glance.*
*He paused. 'My mind better not be playing any tricks.'*
*It definitely was not, in this instance.*

*There it sat, on the kitchen counter.*
*In a vengalapaanai—the smooth, round,*
*pot-bellied brass pot*
*'Aah! This will keep me un-hungry*
*through the winter!*
*Dear, dear Paati, thank you very much. Thanks a lot,*
*For making this pongal and being its inventor.'*

*You know by now Eli's stomach was one big hollow.*
*After the first bite, he reassured his stomach,*

*'Don't worry, there are many more*
*mouthfuls to follow.*
*This is one time I'm not going to hold back.*
*I will keep eating as long as I can swallow.'*

*And so Eli ate. And ate. And ate.*
*He ate up a quarter of the pongal in one go.*
*Would he be able to finish the entire pot?*
*Absolutely no debate!*
*Without a pause, he took a big, no, a humongo ...*
*What's that word?—humongous bite*
*the size of a plate.*

*Now, as you have been observing,*
*The pongal was fast disappearing from the pot.*
*Eli was now onto his third serving*
*And showing no signs of moving from that spot.*
*You may ask, 'So much pongal for one rat?*
*Truly deserving?'*

*We'll have to leave that discussion for another day.*
*Right now, something else was happening.*
*Eli was devouring the pongal, tucking it all away.*
*With all that food, let's just say his senses*

*were not sharpening.*
*Oh, and it wouldn't be any time soon that he'd be able to dance or sashay.*

*At the very beginning of this story, if you remember,*
*Eli's stomach was hollow, unlike the vengalapaanai with the pot belly.*
*What month is it now—never mind—it might as well be September.*
*The pot was still round, but now, so was Eli.*
*He had eaten enough to last him through December!*

## Malli Poo

The jasmine flower or mogra is a quintessential part of Tamil life, used as hair adornments, garlands and religious offerings. It is beloved for its beauty and scent as a symbol of love, grace and purity.

# Nila, Nila, Odi Vaa

Once upon a time, in a far, far place, there lived the Moon Children. As you can guess, the place they lived in was called the Moon Kingdom.

The Moon Children were ageless. Their secret? They were always happy, singing and dancing in the moonlight. One song in particular was their absolute favourite, and everyone in the Moon Kingdom knew and loved it.

I know you will love it too.

This particular night, when the Moon Children began singing and dancing in the grove, it was a chaturdashi of the Krishna Paksha—the fourteenth day of the new moon phase.

*Nila, Nila, odi vaa.*
Moon, O Moon, come, come running!
*Nillamal odi vaa.*
Don't stop on the way, come running!
*Malai mel eri vaa.*
Climb up over the hill and come.

*Malligai pu konduvaa.*

Bring us some jasmine on the way.

*Nadu veetil vei.*

Put them in our courtyard.

*Nalla tithi sei.*

And bring us all good auspices.

Laughing and clapping, the Moon Children went off to their homes. The Moon, listening from above, beamed with joy at her children.

Now, while all this was happening, the ruler of the neighbouring kingdom happened to be passing by. He saw the happy-go-lucky Moon Children. He heard their joyous singing and saw their gleeful dancing. And then he saw the Moon's beaming face. He wanted to experience that same joy, that same delirious happiness. And the way to experience it all was to take the source of all that joy with him, back to his own kingdom.

He ordered his soldiers to capture the Moon and take her back with him to his home.

Tying the Moon to their horses, the soldiers dragged her back with them.

It took them all night to reach their kingdom. Now, the king was—like most kings of that time—

selfish, always wanting to get whatever he felt like. But he was not cruel.

'I'm sure the journey would have been tiring for the Moon. Let her rest during the day. She can beam joy to us after she is well-rested.'

Then he retired to his chambers and was soon royally snoring away. He woke up after a while and went about his kingly duties, like on any other day.

But he couldn't wait for the day to end soon enough. He had the gleaming Moon waiting for him, after all. The Moon! The more he thought about it, the more impatient he became for dusk to arrive.

At last, the last petition for the day was heard in court and disposed of. The king could stop work now. He was, well, not quite over the moon with anticipation, but you can sense how excited he was, can't you?

He eagerly stepped out of the palace and ... was greeted by a bright sun, still shining high in the sky.

The king stopped in his tracks.

'What is this?' he asked his ministers, who were walking alongside him. 'Haven't we been working all through the day? Isn't it time for sunset yet?'

His ministers were as clueless as he was. They looked at each other, perplexed.

'There should be someone who can answer me. Are you all struck dumb?' the king thundered.

It finally occurred to one minister as to who might have the answer.

'Your majesty, surely our kulaguru, the revered teacher of the dynasty, should know the answer to your question. After all, he is well-versed in all fields of knowledge, including the sun and the Moon,' he proffered.

'Call the kulaguru immediately,' ordered the king.

Now, it just happened that the kulaguru was part of the king's entourage that day. He did not want to miss seeing the Moon at close quarters, having heard about how the king had brought her with him to the kingdom the night before.

But now, observing this puzzling solar phenomenon, he wished he had been elsewhere. He had no clue about this un-set sun.

Like the sun, he too had no place to hide. He was ushered in front of the king.

'Well,' asked the king, 'do you have an explanation for this?'

The kulaguru hemmed and hawed and said, 'Your majesty, I will have to consult the astrological charts before I can answer.'

All he wanted to do was buy himself some time; he didn't think there was an answer in the charts.

'Well, do so right away then,' said the king.

The kulaguru pulled out the day's charts, and his face immediately lit up with the first thing he saw. 'Why?', reflected, 'if  if yesterday was chaturdashi, today is ammavasya—the day of the new moon!'

Out loud, the kulaguru said, 'Sire, it is simplicity itself. Today, being ammavasya, the Moon will definitely not put in an appearance. It is just not possible.'

'That is true. Our guru is so wise,' nodded all the ministers. 'He spotted the thing that none of us could see.'

'Fine, I will wait until tomorrow for her to rise,' the king decided and retired to his royal chambers. It didn't occur to him or any of the others to ask one other question.

*While ammavasya explains why the moon was not rising that day, what explains why the sun didn't set at all?*

Anyway, I'm sure all the ministers were happy that it didn't occur to any of them. Or else they would have another question from the king that they couldn't answer. And that would mean they would have to spend a sleepless ... wait, was it still night if the sun didn't set?

The next day, the king and everyone else in the kingdom woke up and went about their duties. Again, the sun showed no signs of setting. Nor was there any sign of the moon.

Dark clouds had gathered, as if a thunderstorm would break out any minute.

The king summoned the kulaguru again.

'What do your charts say today, O Guru?' asked the king.

'Your majesty, there is no need to consult the charts at all. Look at the looming black clouds. How can the Moon have any chance of rising with them clouding around her? Besides, she's still in her new moon phase.'

This kept the king at bay for the day, and he once again retired to his chambers.

As he woke up the next day, it finally occurred to him that while the Moon had not risen, the sun had not set at all through the night.

'Enough!' he said, throwing back the bed covers. 'Take me to the Moon right now. I will order her to rise right away!'

He quickly dressed and went with his retinue to the round room where the Moon was kept.

'O Moon,' the king thundered, 'I'm not going to put up with your tricks and tantrums. Rise now, I order you! Show us your face!'

His order was met with silence.

'O Moon,' the ministers took up a chorus, 'do you know who is addressing you? He is the lord of this realm. You have to obey him!'

The Moon continued to remain unmoved.

When this didn't work, the king tried to cajole the Moon into agreeing to rise.

'O Most Beautiful One, won't you show us your exquisite face? We all so yearn to see you, the one who is unmatched in her beauty by anything else in this universe.'

He might as well have been talking to a distant rock, for there was still no response from the Moon. When neither royal order nor royal entreaty worked, the king thought it was time to threaten the Moon into obeying his command.

But he was stumped on that count, too. What can you actually threaten the Moon with?

Meanwhile, by now, it was the third consecutive day that the sun had not set on the kingdom.

Wells had started to dry up. People's throats were parched. They were finding it difficult to work under the scorching sun. Sleep was eluding them because now there was no night.

Day after day, the sun never set, and the Moon—refusing to obey the king—never rose.

Soon, there was a drought-like condition in the kingdom.

The king was at his wits' end.

Finally, one of the soldiers—the youngest boy in the army—who had been there when the king ordered the Moon to be brought to his kingdom, spoke up.

He had been very upset when the king had

captured the Moon. But what could he do or say? He was a mere boy in the king's vast army.

Today, he finally decided to speak up.

'Your majesty,' he piped up, from his position in the rear of the king's guard, 'if I may ...'

The king looked around to see who had spoken. His ministers and the kulaguru had run out of ideas. He spotted the young boy and called him forward.

'Speak up, boy. What do you have to say?'

'Your majesty,' the boy said, 'I observe that the Moon doesn't obey anyone. She does only what pleases her. And what pleases her is hearing her Moon Children sing and seeing them dance. Perhaps if you requested the Moon Children to sing and dance, the Moon will rise again.'

'That is true!' said the king. 'Let us go at once and request the Moon Children.'

Now, even though the king had taken away their beloved Moon from them, the Moon Children bore no grudges. They were joyous and happy on the inside.

When the king requested them to sing and dance so the Moon would rise again, they readily accepted his request.

You know what they sang as they danced, right?

*Nila, Nila, odi vaa.*

Moon, O Darling Moon, come, come running!

*Nillamal odi vaa.*

Don't stop on the way, come running!

*Malai mel eri vaa.*

Climb up over the hill and come.

*Malligai pu konduvaa.*

Bring us some jasmine on the way.

Suddenly, the air was filled with the fragrance of jasmine. And there was the Moon, rising over the hill, radiant with joy upon seeing her children singing and dancing.

The king realised his folly and begged the Moon for forgiveness.

The Moon, reunited with her beloved Moon Children, forgave the king and went back to spreading silvery joy everywhere.

And that's how they all lived happily ever after.

# What Colour Is Your Favourite Kitten?

'Paati, Paati,' said little Meghana, tugging at her grandmother's sari, 'you have four children. Who's your favourite among them, and how did you decide on that?'

Now, little Meghana might only have been nine years old, but she had posed a very tricky question to Paati.

Come to think of it, when parents have more than one child, how do they decide who their favourite is? And how do they do it without the others feeling bad about it?

I don't know about you, but I certainly want to know how Paati dealt with it, and how she answered little Meghana's question.

'Well, let's see now. Do you know why your Uncle Shyam was named that?' Paati asked.

'I don't know, Paati. Is it because Krishna is your favourite God?' rejoined Meghana.

'Well, that's certainly a good guess, and the answer is related to Krishna, but not because he's my favourite God. Your uncle Shyam was born at dusk, with a dusky complexion, which is what "shyam" means in Sanskrit. And yes, that's what the name "Krishna'' means too.'

'Ooh! I didn't know that!' squealed Meghana, with the excitement of learning something new about her uncle.

'Being the youngest of the four, he was certainly the most pampered, both by me and by his siblings. His elder siblings saw him as a new toy. They simply adored the little boy and loved keeping him engaged and playing with him,' Paati continued. 'He was easily the naughtiest among them. Do you know what his favourite pastime was?'

'What, Paati?' cried Meghana, her eyes shining with curiosity.

'Back then, our house had an old wooden rocking horse. The unique thing about this toy was that his tail would detach from his body, leaving a gaping hole in his, well, behind!' guffawed Paati, wiping tears of laughter as she recalled this vivid memory. 'Now, your Uncle Shyam, mind you—he was

just a little boy back then—he would detach the tail and then drop things into the rocking horse through the hole in its bottom. Oh, the things he would put in there. Spoons, tops, spools of thread, his rattle. Once he even put a whole laddoo through it!'

By now, Meghana was rolling on the floor with laughter. She could just picture her Uncle Shyam as a naughty boy, grabbing things in his tiny, chubby hands and then putting them inside the rocking horse.

'Before I could scold him for his antics, his thatha—your great grandfather—would immediately come to his rescue. "Why are you scolding the child for just being a child? You don't worry, I'll keep an eye out for him and make sure he doesn't hurt himself," Thatha would reassure me. And so the rocking horse continued to receive many more offerings. Why, one Deepavali, your Uncle Shyam put some yummy appam and cheedai into the horse. I doubt that the horse was able to digest them!' Paati continued, giggling away.

'Tell me about my Amma now,' said Meghana, after she and Paati had managed to control their laughter at her Uncle Shyam's childhood antics.

'I'm sure she's your favourite, just like she's my favouritest person in the whole world!'

'Oh, so I'm not your favouritest person in the world, am I?' Paati teased Meghana. But upon seeing the alarm on little Meghana's face, she quickly added, 'I'm just pulling your leg, my dear. Mothers are always their children's favouritest people, and that's how it should be.'

'Well,' she continued, 'let's see now. Your mother, Shweta, was named that because she was born on a sunny winter morning. Bright, pure, fair and full of possibilities—she has lived up to every one of those traits. She has also always been among the fastest, even among her siblings. Your uncles, Lava and Kusha, are older than her, but she was always swifter than them too.'

'Wow!' exclaimed Meghana, once again discovering something she didn't know about her favouritest person in the world. 'Amma was the fastest, even among boys?'

'Her brain is still the fastest, and I bet she can beat your uncles in a race even today,' Paati said, pride for her darling daughter apparent in her words and in her shining eyes. 'When they were all children, nobody could catch her in a game of tag, and she would run circles around all of them!'

'Paati,' Meghana wondered, 'I now understand the logic behind Uncle Shyam's and Amma's names. And I know my elder uncles, Lava and Kusha, are named after Rama's sons. But what do their names mean, and why did you choose those names for them?

'Like Rama's sons, your Lava and Kusha are also twins. They are identical in every respect except for one. Lava has a golden white complexion, while Kusha is dusky, like Rama and like your Uncle Shyam,' Paati replied. 'They are both named after the sacred darba grass, and stand tall, pure and auspicious like its beautiful blades.

'And who was the naughtier among them?' Meghana asked, bubbling with curiosity.

'Now that's a difficult question,' Paati said, with a twinkle in her eye. 'They were equally naughty! Their favourite pastime, as soon as they learnt to walk, was to take whatever they could lay their hands on and drop it into the well in our backyard.

'Oh, my lord!' Paati continued, tears of laughter pooling around her eyes. 'When the gardener came by to draw water from the well, he would have to first retrieve all the things Lava and Kusha had thrown into it.'

'Paati, all of your children sound equally naughty, bright and fun!' Meghana chirped. 'But you still haven't answered my question. Who is your favourite among them?'

'My darling,' Paati replied, 'let me tell you a little story.'

'Ooh, one more story! I love this,' squealed Meghana in excitement.

Instead of just narrating the story, Paati began to sing it.

*There was a white cat*
*Who grew up in our house*
*That white cat*
*Gave birth to a bunch of kittens*
*Of different colours*
*One kitten was charcoal grey*
*Another kitten was black as kajal*
*One kitten was mottled like a snake*
*Another was white like milk*
*But whichever colour each was,*

*You couldn't say one colour was lesser*
*or another greater*
*There were all equally kittens.*

'Now,' Paati continued, 'do you understand who was my favourite among my four children?'

## Payasam

A traditional and simple dessert made of milk, sugar or jaggery and rice (sometimes substituted with sago or vermicelli), garnished with cashews, cardamom and raisins.

# Can a Donkey Tell Camphor's Smell?

There once lived a famous detective called Mookanathan. Mooku, as he was sometimes called, had a nose for knowing everything by its smell.

One sniff, and he could tell what was cooking. In the house. Between people. In the king's palace. Anywhere.

'Ah,' he said, as he passed Uma and Badri's house, 'looks like there is only plain porridge on the menu today. Surely husband and wife have fought this morning.'

Sitting inside, Uma and Badri looked sheepishly at each other. If a passer-by could guess their domestic quarrel with such confidence, how silly they must look. At that thought, they immediately made up with each other.

'Ohohohoho!' Mooku exclaimed, as he crossed Kanjan, the miser's, door. 'Surely he has won the lottery today. Why, he is actually toasting cashews

in real ghee to top up his payasam. Will wonders never cease?'

Kanjan was alarmed at a passing stranger finding out about his windfall.

'Now all the relatives and friends I have never ever heard of will land up at my threshold and ask for money! I knew I should have refrained from using real ghee to toast the cashews,' he wailed.

'Aaah aaah aaah-choo!' Mookanathan sneezed as he passed Paati's yard. 'The monkeys must have stolen a good chunk of the mangoes she had left out to dry yesterday. She's put triple the amount of red chilli powder on them today.'

Now, the king and queen of the land had a child who had just turned a year old. To celebrate this joyous occasion, they declared a celebration for everyone in the kingdom. Any time during the prince's birthday week, everyone was welcome to the palace to enjoy a grand meal and all kinds of goodies.

People came from far and wide and left praising the little prince and his generous parents, the king and queen.

'Ahahaha!' they said in delight, 'the jalebi was so crispy and sweet. I still cannot stop licking my fingers.'

'Ohohoho! The gulab jamun felt like the whole globe was dipped in the most delicious syrup!!' another feaster exclaimed.

'The murukku and cheedai and thattai were so crunchy and wholesome, I could not stop eating them,' cried another happy partaker of the birthday feast.

As you can imagine, all kinds of people came into the palace that week. Rich, poor, young, old, farmers, artisans, musicians, craftspeople, dancers, blacksmiths, carpenters, merchants, sailors and so many more flocked to the week-long celebration.

Apart from the feast for their taste buds and their stomach, there was one other thing every visitor came away praising.

The young prince was wearing a golden bracelet that had a single red ruby. The gem sparkled like the eye of the sun, and everyone who saw it was dazzled.

'The prince is as radiant as the ruby on his wrist!' they all agreed.

Alas, on the seventh day of the birthday week, the ruby bracelet got stolen.

Now you may wonder how anyone could steal

such a precious thing from the royal prince's wrist, especially when there were so many people around.

But it was precisely because there were so many people around that the theft went unnoticed.

As much as they were shocked at the theft, people were also awestruck by the audacity of such a daring act that happened in broad daylight, right under the very nose of the king and the queen.

'Who knows who stole the bracelet? It's going to be impossible to find out,' said one of the visitors.

The king immediately knew who he had to call.

You guessed it. Mookanathan.

Now, Mookanathan's success and fame came at a price. There were plenty of people who scoffed at his 'special talent' and thought he was just fooling everyone.

'What's the big deal about smelling things? Anyone with a nose can do it,' thought the fuming grand vizier, jealous of the king calling Mooku to solve the mystery instead of getting him to look into the matter.

Aloud, he said, 'Your majesty, there is no need to bother sending for Mookanathan. I can solve this crime and catch the culprit in no time at all. By the time Mooku gets here, the thief will be far away. We have no time to waste.'

The king looked at his grand vizier and said, 'By all means, do your best, but I will send for Mooku regardless. He immediately knows when something is fishy.'

'Fishy!' thought the grand vizier. 'Ah, now I know how Mooku solves mysteries! If something smells fishy, then it must be fishy. I just need to follow my nose for anything suspicious.'

Once again, aloud, he simply said, 'Leave it to me, your majesty. I will sniff out the thief in no time at all!'

So, while the grand vizier took his nose and himself in search of the thief, the king sent for Mooku, who arrived to see a hilarious sight: the grand vizier, strutting about the palace, sticking his nose close to people.

'Ah! You smell fishy!' said the grand vizier. Then, clutching the arm of a well-built young man, he shouted, 'Out with it. Confess that you are the thief.'

'Are you mad?' replied that young man. 'I smell fishy because I am a fisherman. What else would I smell of? Onions?'

The room burst out with laughter.

Red-faced, the grand vizier moved on farther and stopped at a portly pot-bellied man who let out a big burp just as the grand vizier reached him.

'Eww!' the grand vizier cringed. 'You smell of onions. And you certainly don't look like an onion-seller. Ha, surely you are the thief!'

'Begone!' said the pot-bellied man. 'I smell of onions because I just had the biggest plate of the best onion pakodas in the world. And what you smelt is my onion pakoda burp.'

So saying, he let out another enormous burp in the grand vizier's face, who quickly ran away to another corner of the palace's Grand Hall.

'Let me put this poor man out of his misery,' thought Mooku and went up to the king.

'Your majesty, the grand vizier is looking in the wrong place to solve this mystery. May I first see the prince up close?' he asked.

'Of course,' the king replied, and took Mooku to the prince.

Mooku picked up the chubby little prince, all round and pink as babies his age are supposed to be. The toddler was blissfully unaware of all the drama happening around him and had been playing with his silver rattle filled with all kinds of precious stones.

Mooku noticed that the prince's hands were extra soft, smoother than a baby's hands usually are. He smiled and bent down as if to kiss the prince on his cheek.

'Your majesty,' Mooku said. 'I believe the young prince loves butter.'

'He does,' said the king, astonished. 'But how did you know that?'

'No matter, your majesty,' replied Mooku. 'Could you ask the royal cowherd to personally bring his young highness a handful of the creamiest butter right away?'

A few minutes later, the royal cowherd was ushered into the Grand Hall.

Mooku greeted him politely and asked, 'O royal cowherd, what is that in your hand?'

The king and the other onlookers were puzzled at Mooku's question. Wasn't he the one who had asked the royal cowherd to bring the creamiest butter for the young prince?

The cowherd was equally puzzled.

'Dear sir,' he replied, 'it is the butter that you requested for the young prince.'

'No, no, my dear royal cowherd,' Mooku said, his voice silken like creamy butter, 'I meant in your other hand, where the ruby cut into your palm?'

'What? The prince's ruby never touched my palm, it was always facing the other way ...' The cowherd stopped mid-sentence, panic-stricken upon realising what he had just said.

Knowing he was caught, the cowherd fell to his knees and begged the king for forgiveness.

'Pardon me, O all-knowing one,' he pleaded to Mooku. 'I stole the bracelet in a moment of weakness. I meant no harm! Here it is. I regret the moment I took it. Please forgive me.'

'I'm not the one to seek forgiveness from. It is for the king to decide your fate,' replied Mooku, handing the bracelet over to the king.

While the guards took the cowherd away, the king—and all the onlookers, the grand vizier included—were astonished at Mooku's genius.

'But how did you know it was the cowherd, Mooku?' asked the king.

'It was simplicity itself, your majesty,' said Mooku. 'When I picked up the prince, I noticed his hands were extra smooth, as if he had just had some butter. And when I bent down to kiss him, I picked up the distinctive smells found around a Cowherd: grass, cows, milk and butter. I knew that no one but the royal Cowherd would have permission to personally give butter to the prince. He simply slipped the bracelet off the prince's wrist with his buttery fingers. I didn't want him to know that I suspected him, so I simply asked him to bring some more butter for the prince. You heard his confession. That's all there is to it.'

The grand vizier came up to Mookanathan with folded hands and said, 'I was a vain fool to think I could match your genius. Having a nose is no qualification to do what you just did. After all, *kazhuthaiku theriyuma karpoora vasanai?* Can a donkey tell camphor's smell?!'

# The Crow and the Medu Vada

In the big kitchen behind the royal banquet hall, a feast was being prepared. Huge vats of food stood steaming even while being covered with lids. What delicious dishes they hid!

Now, don't you wrinkle up your nose hearing that aviyal is one of those delicious dishes, just because it has all kinds of vegetables in it. Once you take a bite, you won't even know you're eating so many veggies. Yes, yes, you, and I both know it has vendakaai and beans and murungakaai (the moringa seeds are so yummy!). And it also has potatoes (ooooh!) and chepankazhangu. And lots of coconut. And spicy green chillies. And cooling yoghurt. Anyway, it's really tasty. Try it.

What else was there in those huge containers? There was sambar and rasam. Ooh, roasted potatoes. What's not to like about them? And banana chips, freshly made. And tangy, newly made diced mango

pickle. Fried papad. Beans poriyal sprinkled with grated coconut. I'm losing track of the number of dishes now. And the cooks are still at it, making even more items.

What's that sizzling in that big pan now?

Medu vada!

Crispy, round, bites of savoury heaven. That's what I think medu vadas are.

The cook had dropped enough batter in the pan to make just one medu vada. He scooped it out of the pan with a ladle and examined it with an expert eye.

'Ah! Just the right golden-brown colour and perfectly crisp,' he thought. The oil was now hot enough to make big batches of medu vada at a time.

He dropped the 'test' medu vada—perfect as it was—into a basket where the extra oil would drain into a pan placed underneath it. He then started taking handfuls of batter and putting little scoops of them, one at a time, into the pan until over forty medu vadas were sizzling away in the oil.

The cook walked away from the pan, knowing they would take a few minutes to be fried to perfection. And he forgot all about the test medu vada in the basket.

All this while, Karu the crow had been perched on the banyan tree opposite the kitchen. This was just the moment he was waiting for.

Quick as a flash, he flew from the tree, picked up the medu vada in his beak and darted into the sky. He flew a little distance, away from the banquet hall and the palace and into the thick forest at the edge of the city.

There he found a tree with a broad bough and sat down on it.

Now, a jackal who was in the vicinity had been eyeing Karu. To be more specific, he was eyeing the medu vada in the crow's mouth. Jackals, as a rule, have no interest in crows. Crows are too high up and too swift to become a jackal's prey.

But this crow was different. The jackal had spotted him just as he came swooping out of the city and into the forest. What caught his attention was that the crow had something in his mouth. At first, he thought it might be a mouse that the bird had snatched from outside a house. Then his eyes glinted with delight—for he had discerned that the crow was carrying a most unexpected but utterly desirable treat.

His cunning brain immediately set to work.

As soon as the crow settled on the bough of the tree, the jackal cleared his throat and, in his most polite voice, said, 'Karu, Karu, your sleek black coat looks extra elegant today. And I look at your shapely throat and immediately imagine how sweet the song must be that comes from it! Won't you please sing me a song?'

Flattery, as you know, will get you almost anything.

In this case, Karu the crow melted at the jackal's pure admiration. Forgetting what he had in his mouth, he opened it to give his sole audience a sample of his musical talent.

Out popped the medu vada and fell to the ground before he could get the first caw out of his throat.

The jackal was in a perfect position to catch the snack before it touched the ground and accepted it gleefully. And as soon as he caught his prize, he heard a human voice behind him.

'Well caught, jackal!' the voice said. 'That was very clever of you.'

Alarmed at a human having gotten so near him, the jackal sprinted deeper into the forest with the medu vada in his mouth. He turned around to check that there was no one on his tail.

'Ah, now to sit in peace and enjoy my medu vada,' he said aloud to himself.

'Indeed, little jackal,' growled a tiger's voice from the brush. 'I wish I had a medu vada too.'

Almost frightened out of his skin, the jackal took to his heels once again. Out of breath, he still clutched the medu vada in his mouth and ran until he found a small clearing in the woods. He paused there and looked around.

'No humans or tigers here, thank goodness!' he said.

The jackal paused and waited for a few moments, just in case someone else appeared on the scene. When nothing happened, he heaved a sigh of relief.

And then a voice spoke.

Oh, what a sweet voice it was. The most captivating voice the jackal had ever heard.

It was a she-jackal's voice.

'O magnificent one with the medu vada in his mouth,' she crooned, 'your pointy ears, your bushy tail and your sleek body are a sight to behold by themselves. But that medu vada in your mouth, that tells me even more about you. If you got it from a human kitchen without people noticing you, then you are daring and sharp. And if you got it from another creature who got it from the humans, that tells me you're cleverer than most.'

The jackal couldn't see who was speaking, but he was mesmerised by the voice. Still, he couldn't reply because he had the medu vada in his mouth.

'Do you want to see me, o jackal?' the voice continued. 'All you have to do is call out my name. Just say Meena, and I'll come to you.'

'This is my lucky day,' the jackal thought. 'I'll have my medu vada with Meena.'

And so he opened his mouth—dropping the medu vada—and called out in his jackal-y voice, 'MeEeENaAaaaa!'

And who should swoop in but Meena the myna! Quicker than the jackal's brain could understand what had just transpired, Meena the myna picked up the medu vada that had dropped from the jackal's mouth and flew up to a tree where her friend, Karu the crow, was sitting.

All that the jackal could do was gape in open-mouthed astonishment.

Where had the sweet she-jackal whose lovely voice he had heard just a moment ago vanished?

'I'm right here, o puzzled jackal,' came the she-jackal's voice, as if reading his mind.

The jackal looked up to the tree, because that's where the voice was coming from.

'That's right,' continued Meena the myna in the she-jackal's voice, 'it's me! I'm your she-jackal.'

And then quickly changing her voice, she growled, 'And I'm also your tiger.'

The jackal jumped, hardly able to believe his own ears.

'Remember,' Meena the myna continued, this time in a human's voice, 'before you jump out of your skin again, you better tuck your tail between your legs and run away before I catch you!'

And that's exactly what the jackal did.

'Oh, Meena,' Karu said, with great gratitude in

his voice, 'I knew that mynas can mimic anyone's voice, but you were so convincing that I too thought that a she-jackal, a tiger and a human had all climbed this tree and were sitting next to me! Thank you for saving the medu vada from the jackal's jaws. Won't you please join me in eating it?'

And that's how Karu and Meena snatched the medu vada from the jaws of the jackal and enjoyed their feast on the tree. I wish I could get a bite of it too!

## Oonjal

Less commonly seen now, this wooden swing hanging from the ceiling on sturdy iron chains was a central part of most Tamil homes, serving as furniture and as the family gathering space. The oonjal is still a core part of Tamil wedding rituals, symbolising life's ups and downs.

# Muthu's Guide to Basic Maths

*There was once a little boy*
*Who could turn anything into a toy.*
*His name, if you must know, was Muthu*
*And he was anything but a buddhu.*

*He turned a crooked stick into a catapult*
*And created a whole lot of tumult.*
*He took a rough, round stone*
*And rubbed it until it shone.*

*He whittled a big fat twig*
*And turned it into a twirling, dizzying top.*
*He took birds' feathers and created a wig*
*Oh, you just couldn't get Muthu to stop.*

*He found a shallow little bog*
*In which swam a slithery tadpole.*

*He said, 'Oh, you little not-yet-frog,*
*You do burrow through water like a mole!'*

*He found an ancient banyan tree*
*On which hung a hornet's nest.*
*He stirred it and yelled, 'I'm setting you free!'*
*He got stung and said, 'Leaving it alone might have been best.'*

*Our dear little Muthu could never leave anything alone*
*But ask him to count any number*
*Even if it was just the very first one,*
*And for the life of him, he couldn't remember.*

*So who should he go to but his dear old Paati?*
*She always seems to have, for every question, an answer.*
*Paati might be old, but she's still a big smarty!*
*Muthu took his math problem and approached her.*

*'Paati, Paati, I can't tell three from eight*
*And I don't know how many are nine.*

*How do I get my numerals right?*
*I can do everything else just fine.'*

*Wise old Paati was a whiz*
*In using rhyme with reason.*
*Why, I bet Muthu could even win a quiz,*
*Once he learnt from her the singing numeric lesson.*

*Paati knew that Muthu knew about everything*
*Even if he couldn't tell one digit from another.*
*Would you like to hear her sing*
*The mnemonic numerical song*
*she learnt from her mother?*

*This is how it went*
*And for Muthu, it was heaven-sent!*
*It connected numbers with the things Muthu knew*
Many, many things, not just a few.

'One, you have one head
Two, you have two eyes on your one face
Three, a tripod has three legs
Four, a chair has four legs

Five, your hand has five fingers
Six, a fly has six legs
Seven, a week has seven days
Eight, a spider has eight legs
Nine, there are nine types of grains
Ten, two hands have ten fingers.'

Muthu marvelled at Paati's ditty.
'From now on, I will always have this in my kitty!
*Now I won't ever forget how many are six.*
*With numbers, I'll never again be in a fix!'*

# The Jalebi Judge

You know what the best part of a jalebi is? Yes, yes, I like it too when it's super crunchy, and the sweeter it is, the yummier it tastes. I agree with you.

But that's not the best part of a jalebi. It's the sticky but not-at-all-icky sugar syrup that bursts out when you bite into it.

Slurrrppp!!!

Oh, I'm not the only one who thinks that's the best part of a jalebi.

One day, two spiders—Poochi and Poochu—were dangling from the branch of a tree, lazily spinning their silky yarn behind them, like two trapeze artistes just hanging out. They were best friends, and like best friends, they did everything together.

Sitting under the tree was the town's confectioner, taking a break on his journey to the next village to sell his treats. He had set down his basket full of sweets next to him, while he leaned against the tree to stretch his legs and take a quick nap.

Poochi's and Poochu's sixteen eyes (between them) bulged with excitement! They moved their sixteen legs (between them) faster to get themselves closer to the gleaming jalebis in the confectioner's basket.

'Look at that juicy jalebi! Let's go grab it before he wakes up!' squealed Poochi to Poochu.

'I can't wait to sink my straw into it!' whispered Poochu, barely able to get his voice out in excitement.

Silently, they slithered down on their silky yarn, landing on either side of a jalebi in the man's basket. Grasping it with eight legs apiece, they lifted themselves back up on their yarn and settled on a high branch, out of sight of the sleeping confectioner.

After a while, the man woke up, stretched himself and went his way.

With no risk of anyone bothering them now, Poochi and Poochu turned their attention to the jalebi.

Now, with most food items, it would be easy enough to divide them into equal halves. You can cut a round appam in half from any part of its diameter. You can do the same with a globe-like gulab jamun. You can even cut a laddoo in half.

But how do you divide a squiggly, wriggly, convoluted jalebi into equal parts? More importantly, how can you tell which part has more of the sublime sugar syrup?

This was the question Poochi and Poochu were confronted with now.

Greedy to enjoy the jalebi quickly, they forgot the first rule of being best friends: that it doesn't matter if one of them got a little more than the other. Instead, they started bickering among themselves.

'I saw the jalebi first with my eight googly eyes!' claimed Poochi.

'So what? I was the first one to reach and touch it with my seventh leg!' retorted Poochu.

'I was the one who introduced you to the delightful pleasure of jalebis. Otherwise, your diet would only consist of flies even today,' said Poochi.

'You may have shown me a jalebi first, but I was the one who discovered the yummy sugar syrup inside it to slurp!' replied Poochu.

And so they kept arguing with each other.

Korangu the monkey was observing their bickering from a nearby branch. His eye—no points for guessing—was on the jalebi. He didn't need eight eyes to spot an opportunity. Just two were enough.

'Come, come,' he intervened. 'You are best friends. You can't be fighting like this. You must trust each other.'

'I will trust him if he trusts me,' said Poochi.

'You look like a wise monkey. Can you tell us how to resolve this?' asked Poochu.

'It will be my pleasure to help two best friends,' offered Korangu. All the while, he kept thinking, 'Oh, and I'll help myself too!'

'Now, it doesn't matter who does it, but can one of you divide the jalebi into two halves? I'll make sure they are equal,' said Korangu.

Poochi graciously handed the jalebi to Poochu and said, 'Go ahead. You divide it into two halves.'

Poochu broke the jalebi into two parts with his four forelegs.

Alas, a jalebi doesn't lend itself to being divided into equal, symmetrical halves. One part was larger than the other.

'No matter,' said Korangu. 'I will make these two parts equal.'

He took the part that was larger and took a small bite out of it.

'Now they should both be equal,' he said.

But what is this? The previously smaller part was now larger!

'No matter,' said Korangu once again. 'I'll make this right.'

And he took a bite from the now larger part.

Now that part became smaller, and the other part became larger in comparison.

This continued, and before Poochi and Poochu could realise it, Korangu had polished off the whole jalebi, bit by bit. And off he ran at once, smacking his lips with joy.

Poochi and Poochu were left ruing the fact that they had trusted Korangu to be a jalebi judge instead of just trusting each other.

## Anjarai Petti

Literally meaning a 'five-compartment box,' it is the ubiquitous spice box in every Tamil household that has the essential seasoning and condiments used in everyday cooking.

# The Banana Skiing Contest

There once lived a very wise, not-so-old langur in a forest.

How, you may wonder, if he was not-so-old, did the langur get so wise? He certainly looked the part, with a salt-and-pepper beard and hair framing his calm face. But the real reason he was wise was because he had travelled to places far and wide as well as to places near and narrow.

The forest he lived in was near Rameswaram, a town at the southernmost tip of India. And the nearest and narrowest place he had travelled to was Dhanushkodi, from where, legend has it, his legendary ancestor Hanuman had leapt across the ocean.

Right now, though, he was most excited about the farthest and widest place that he had recently returned from: the Himalayas!

There, he had seen the elusive snow leopard, not visible in any other forest. He had seen an ibex

defying gravity and clinging on sure-footedly to the sides of towering mountains.

But the thing he was most fascinated by—and most excited about too—was snow! Rameswaram, being so close to the equator, has as much chance of snow as there is of a sloth winning a race among all the animals.

What was it about the snow that had him all abuzz with excitement?

It was this thing he had seen humans do there. They strapped their feet onto these flat, long planks. And then off they would whiz—downhill, over crevasses and valleys.

They called it skiing, and they even did it when the ground was flat, not sloping downwards. They called that cross-country skiing, this gliding thing they did. And it was all possible because of the snow. Powdery, soft, smooth and, above all, slippery!

'Wouldn't it be amazing if we could all ski here?' the langur said, his eyes shining with excitement from this vivid memory.

'That's all very well to do up in the Himalayas, dear langur,' said the other animals, 'but how on earth are we going to get snow here in Rameswaram?'

The counter question makes the not-so-old langur appear not-so-wise now, doesn't it?

Oh, don't worry. Wise not-so-old langur had the answer to this question.

'You were not listening very closely to what I said, were you?' he asked the other animals.

The parrot pondered this, his head cocked to one side.

The tortoise withdrew into his shell to shut out all noise and see if he could recall fully what the langur had said.

The hyena hemmed and hawed and harrumphed, but he had no answer either.

The bear scratched his back and his front, his bottom and his top, but found no clue forthcoming.

The deer, that little old dear, oh deer, I daresay she knew nothing either.

'Oh, never mind!' said the langur impatiently. 'Let me just tell you all again.'

'Yes, yes, that will be great,' nodded all the animals gratefully.

'Snow is great for skiing, because it's soft, smooth and, ABOVE ALL, SLIPPERY!' repeated the langur.

The animals waited patiently for the langur to shed a little more light on the subject.

'Don't you see? We just need to make the path soft, smooth and, ABOVE ALL, SLIPPERY. And who knows what it takes to make things slippery more than us monkeys?' said the langur triumphantly.

'Ba ... bananas?' said a baby loris timidly.

'That's right, my baby loris, bananas!' roared the langur.

Now, everyone saw it, and their eyes too gleamed with excitement.

'Yaanai raja,' the langur said, addressing the leader of the elephant herd, 'you love bananas as much as we monkeys do. Let's join forces and bring all the bananas we can gather to Marudhamalai. That hill with arjun trees has the perfect slope to ski from, and it is wide enough for us all to ski together at the same time. It will be a race!'

'A skiing race, that too! What fun!' thought all the animals.

In a week, the elephants, langurs, lorises and bonnet monkeys of the forest had paved the broad slope of Marudhamalai with bananas as far as the eye could see.

They decided to hold the very first skiing race on a full moon night. So what if they didn't have white snow? The bananas would glisten like snow in the silvery moonlight.

And so, at race time, they all stood at the starting line. There was one representative from anteaters, bulbuls and bonnet monkeys; deer, elephants, hares and hyenas; jackals, kites, langurs and lorises; nilgai, owls, parrots, sloths, thrush and warblers.

You can imagine the bedlam that followed.

The anteater's scales got in the way of his sliding down the slippery slope.

The bulbuls, kites, owls, parrots, thrush and warblers all faced the same problem: as birds, they had no clue how to get their legs and wings out of the way and slide on their stomachs. And their bottoms—well, let's just say their bottoms were not made for sliding.

The bonnet monkeys and lorises were too excited to do anything. They chattered non-stop, and not being blessed with baboon bottoms, they were not exactly speeding away either.

The hare, normally fleet of foot, found his natural advantage was of no use when it came to banana skiing. He kept slipping and flipping on his head every few steps, making his progress in the race so slow that he might as well have been an elephant or a tortoise.

The deer, hyena, jackal and nilgai were there just to add to the numbers and posed no serious challenge.

The langur, our not-so-old and wise one, had made a pair of skis for himself. He was faster than the others, but he was quickly learning that banana skiing was very different from snow skiing, even if, ABOVE ALL, both made for slippery slopes.

You have spotted the problem that all the animals were facing. Their instinct was to move their limbs here, there and everywhere—as if they were walking or running or flying or swimming. And that only made things worse for them.

Did I say all animals?

All except one.

It was the one who instinctively knew that the path of least resistance was also the fastest downhill.

There he goes now, zipping past all of them, not moving a limb or hair.

The sloth!

His motionlessness normally means he's not going anywhere in a hurry.

But here, the banana skins took care of moving him. The more still he was, the faster he skied downhill!

Soon, he had left all the other animals behind, even the langur!

The langur didn't mind that he didn't win the race. His banana skiing race was a big hit.

# Acknowledgements

Amma, for giving me these and a childhood filled with stories.

Appa, for instilling in me the ability to always be a child.

Sudha, my sister, for helping with some of the stories but more importantly, for being one of the most ardent believers in my writing abilities.

Vidhi Bhargava, my publisher at Westland, for not forgetting these stories even years after I had first shared them with her and for helping them see the light of day.

Muhammed Lesin, my editor at Westland, for adroitly and unobtrusively showing how much value an editor brings to a book.

Nirzara Verulkar, for brilliantly and visually bringing to life the world of my–and Amma's–imagination in these stories via her vivid illustrations.

My niece Megha, for whom I wrote my first ever children's story–and for treating me (and not just the story) with a wide-eyed fandom that continues to make me believe I'm not a bad storyteller.

And a whole bunch of others who have read my writing over the years–I hope you know how much you have encouraged me without knowing that's what you were doing.

Other book in this series

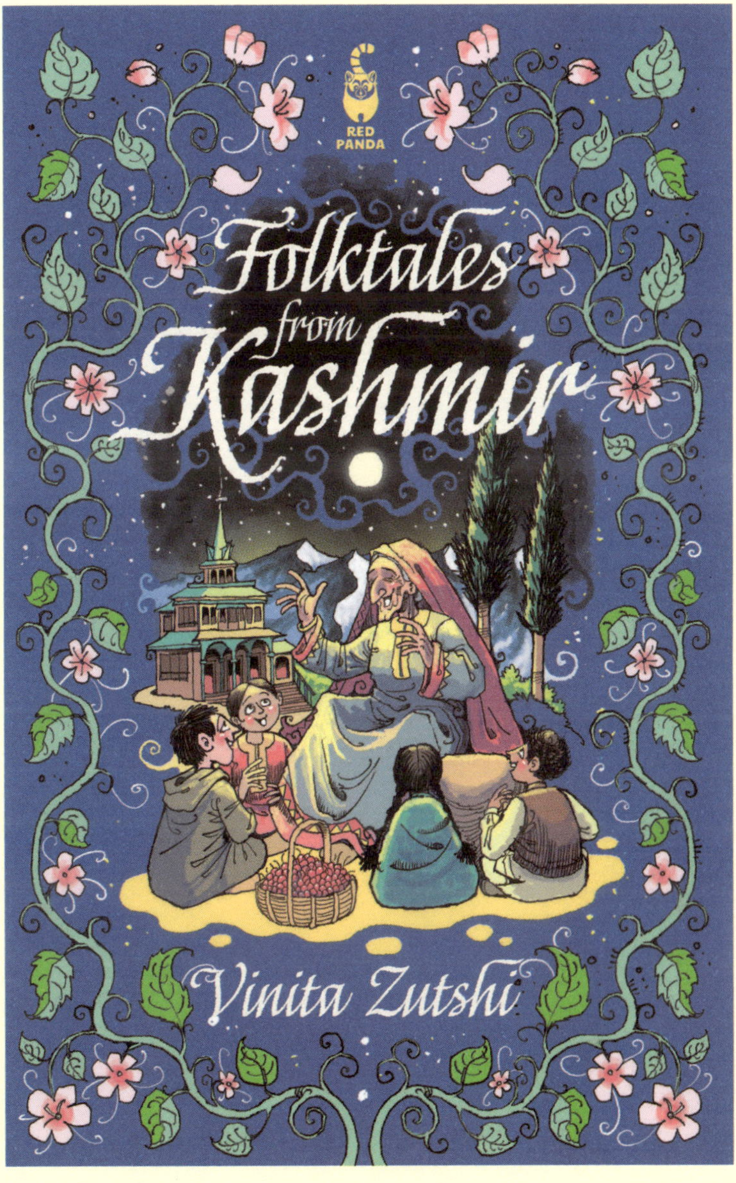